transmission from zero

CHRISTOPHER MICHAEL WEISMAN

Foolish Cat Publishing
Published by Foolish Cat Publishing
34 Birchwood Lane #2
Jackson, TN 38305

First Foolish Cat Publishing February 2010

Printed in the United States of America

Foolish Cat Publishing ISBN: 978-0-615-35165-0

This book is dedicated to my wife, Misty.
If not for her steadfast support, this book would never have come to fruition.

CONTENTS

PROLOGUE

Lt Commander David Johnson ducked his head as he stepped through the final airlock. The airtight hatch slid closed behind him with an audible thump as the negative pressure atmosphere took hold of its weight. He made his way over to his work station on the far end of the room, passing row after row of stainless steel biological safety cabinets on either side.

This is where the ugly ones are kept, David thought to himself as he sat in the sterile steel office chair at his desk. Ebola, Hemorrhagic Fever, Marburg virus, all here. There was a quick hiss as he plugged the air supply hose into the positive air pressure manifold above his head. The sudden change in pressure caused David's hazmat suit to inflate slightly and his ears to pop painfully. He reached a rubber gloved hand up to his ear in a vain attempt to cradle his throbbing head, receiving a handful of rubber suit for his trouble. Irritated at the pain in his ears and his own stupidity, he grumbled a string of profanities under his breath.

Centering his attention again on the task at hand, David looked at the cabinet directly in front of him. The most interesting of all the bugs was located directly on the other side of that cabinet. Although bug is the wrong word, he thought. Bug implies that the organism can replicate, find sustenance and live on its own. No, this is a virus. By definition, it infects a cell and changes the way that it functions. Further, it then uses that host to replicate and then infect more cells. Herpes, AIDS, hell even the Flu are all a pain in the ass, although some more than others.

Most viruses are typically thought of as a detriment to humanity, but not this one, he thought. This could be mankind's greatest discovery. Genetically engineered from the start it would turn out to be a masterpiece, albeit thus far it had a bit of a rough start. Keying in the eight-digit code on the brushed silver panel, David opened the cabinet to a whoosh of rushing air to reveal the hermetically sealed containers within. Reaching in, he withdrew a small oval shaped container and placed it on the tabletop directly below. The top of the container had a white plastic seal which read "H.T.O.V. beta trial A2" and was followed by a string of numbers. David settled onto the cold metal stool before breaking the seal of the container.

HTOV or the Human Terminal Operability Virus was the culmination of David's life work. Keeping his head down, just trudging his way through his coursework, he had graduated top of his class from the Stanford School of Medicine. He had an extremely difficult residency, not because of his skill as a doctor, but from the inability to deal with patients. Patients, even worse their families, would never listen to reason. Every time he had to give a less than optimistic diagnosis, they would start asking questions, demanding answers and screaming for a solution that medical science just couldn't give them. It took all of David's self-restraint not to raise his voice, tell them that this is just the way it is and deal with it! By the end of his residency, he knew that telling old ladies that they had the shingles could never be his career.

After several months of applying to various research firms and pharmaceutical companies, he applied for a job at the Naval Health

Research Center in San Diego. Within months of his arrival, his work was gaining notoriety in the Respiratory Disease Division. Initially hired as a civilian employee by the Navy Department, he decided to apply for a commission in the United States following the urging of several officers with whom he worked after a year of employment. Everyone had informed him in a half joking, half serious manner that this was the only way to play with the "fun" bugs. After several successful years into his commission, he was approached by a severe looking medical corps Captain. David was ushered into a secure conference room, and after a security briefing which included the threat of death by firing squad if any of the information in the presentation was leaked, the plans for the Human Terminal Operability Virus was laid out to him in explicit detail. He would be overseeing the compartmentalized top secret project and in command of a small army of researchers and security. David had decided to accept the position even before the end of the presentation and was on a military transport flight to Tampa by the end of the week.

In his tenth year as project director, the program had made vast leaps forward. While it was true that his team had yet to achieve the project's objectives, the current *setback* excited David even more than the original project goal. There was no way around it; the team had achieved apparent reanimation! David sat back, thinking of the possibilities. True, there didn't seem to be any higher brain function in the revived lab animals, the infection of two researchers was unfortunate, but imagine the implications! He snapped himself out of his revelry and unscrewed the lid from the top of the container. He needed to run a DNA profile on the newest changes engineered to the virus prior to the next round of testing. He reached over and grabbed the test kit. He noted the time as 1525 Hours, entered it into the log, and began the procedure. A moment later, a hurried female voice sounded over the built in speaker in his hazmat suit. "Sir, I have prepped the specimens for the next test. Would you like me to bring them in?"

"In a moment Sharon, I have to complete this and start the sequencing. I don't want any accidental PCR contamination from you or the animals." He replied through internal mic in his suit.

“Okay sir; let me know when you are ready. I am moving the test subjects now and will prep them for the next trial.”

“Very well!” David snapped. Disliked being rushed, he also preferred that airtight doors remain closed while the virus was exposed. Making a mental note to append the operating procedures at the next revision, he sighed to himself, and continued the sampling of the virus.

The room suddenly jumped out from beneath David, violently throwing him off the stool and onto the floor. The lab then shook violently as a deafening rumble filled the air. The Lexan windows of the lab shattered as shockwaves wrenched at the structural integrity of the building. The airtight hatch on the lab blew off its hinges, and a wave of pressure and heat crushed David’s suit. A large piece of reinforced concrete fell onto David, collapsing his chest. The building wrenched again as a cave in the bedrock, located several hundred feet below the structure gave way, forming a sink hole. Half of the underground structure began to collapse into the new crevasse, peeling away the layer of offices, labs and other working areas. As the rumbling began to subside, the wall to the level 4 lab crumbled away, exposing a shaft of light.

CHAPTER ONE

The bright Florida sunshine temporarily blinded Rob as he pulled into the small parking lot and chose one of the vacant parking spaces. He put the Jeep into park and pulled the key from the ignition. Pulling open the door the young man stepped out in front of the non-descript building that housed Brian's company. Unconsciously, Rob reached in to grab his hat and chuckled as he remembered he didn't have to wear one anymore.

Having just gone on terminal leave days before, he was finding that after six years in the Navy old habits were hard to break. Instead, he took a quick inventory of himself. One side of his button down shirt had pulled free and was quickly tucked back into the baggy khaki slacks. This was one of the drawbacks of his build, long arms and broad shoulders made finding correct fitting shirts a pain. He also remembered the pants fitting a bit tighter the last time he wore them. Looking down, the fly of his jeans, belt buckle and seam of his shirt were all in straight alignment. A bead of sweat caused by the oppressive Florida humidity began to run down the side of his head beneath the close-cropped hair.

He wasn't kidding about it being small, he thought as he walked up to the shabby building and opened the door. A blast of cool air greeted him as he entered the lobby.

"Good afternoon, how may I help you?" asked the young woman behind the small desk with fire engine red hair.

"Hello," Rob responded, "is Mr. Watson available?"

"May I ask who is –," she began but was interrupted by a tall figure who stepped out from the back office.

"Holy shit! Is that Rob Cohen I hear?" bellowed a disembodied voice from around the corner. A giant of a man with a surprising graceful gait stepped into view. Easily six and a half feet tall and probably a bit intimidating if one didn't know he was a big teddy bear, the man reached Rob and gave him a huge hug.

"Take it easy there, killer" Rob replied hoarsely as the breath was squeezed out of him and gave the man a quick double pat on the back. As Brian stepped back Rob said, "Nice place you have here, man. But I have to admit I was expecting something a bit more extravagant."

"Yeah, well, you know, it keeps overhead down. That combined with the cheap help…"

"Hey!" the woman said. "I am not cheap!"

"I'll be the judge of that." Brian winked at her. "Rob, I want you to meet my girlfriend and administrative assistant extraordinaire, Tina Banks."

"Nice to meet you." Rob said as he stepped over and shook her hand.

"Brian has told me a lot about you. Most of it from High School and College."

"Aww hell, and you'll still shake hands after hearing all that? You must be a great woman." It was Rob's turn to wink.

"Well, I try to take everything he tells me with a grain of salt, so don't worry. I will reserve my judgment for later." She gave Rob a warm smile.

"Well Honey, we are heading to lunch. I need you to hold down the fort while we are gone." Brian said as he reached over and opened the door for Rob.

"And when can I expect you back?"

"Well," He said and then with a sly grin, "this will be an, ahem, working lunch, so it could take most of the afternoon."

"I figured," She deadpanned, "just gimme a call if you need me to close up so that I am not stuck here all night. I have plans tonight myself."

"Ohh!" Brian mused, "Which boyfriend is it tonight? Raul or Tyrone?"

She huffed and said with a smile, "Wouldn't you like to know!" Then said, "Have fun guys!"

"Love you!" Brian said.

"Nice meeting you, Tina." Rob said as he stepped out the door.

The bright sunlight once again blinded Rob as they stepped into the world outside. Brian walked over to the driver's side of a black BMW, hitting a button on his keychain to unlock the door. Rob walked to the passenger side and opened the door. "A seven series, huh? You *must* have to keep overhead down to afford *this*," he said as he got in.

"We all have our vices," Brian said, getting in and starting the car. As he pulled out, he asked, "So how are you getting along being home?"

"Not bad. I had been staying with my folks but I found a cheap little place out on Davis Islands. I am waiting for the movers to show up with the rest of my stuff." He looked over at Brian. "I have to admit, this place has changed a bit from six years ago."

"No doubt, but, Tampa is Tampa." Brian glanced over to the truck to his left and laughed, "I see that you still have the Jeep."

"Yeah man, you can't beat it! It runs like a dream and it's paid for. What more do you need?"

"One word my friend, S-T-Y-L-E, style! Or at least fake it 'til you make it!" Brian said, lovingly stroking the steering wheel.

"Nahhh, I keep her washed. That's all that matters." Rob said. Brian pulled into parking lot of the small restaurant and Rob's phone rang. He pulled it out as he unbelted himself and opened the door. Looking to Brian he said, "I will meet you in there." Brian nodded as Rob answered the phone.

"Hello," he spoke into the phone as he looked across the parking lot at the traffic on the avenue.

"Hey! I am up at the base for drill weekend. What are you up to tonight?" The female voice on the other end said.

"I don't have any plans right now, Sarah. I am just going to eat lunch with Brian."

"Humph, well, we are going out tonight. I'm thinking, Channelside?"

"Sure, what time do you get off?"

"Well, Rob that depends on y—"

"You know what I mean." He interrupted and then sighed, "I have only been in town for 3 days and already you start in." He smiled, "Give me a call when you're done. You can meet me at my place, I'll give you directions later."

"Ok, sure. Gotta run, I will see you later Rob." She said hurriedly.

"Bye," Rob replied and slid the phone back into his front pocket.

Rob stepped into the restaurant and was immediately hit with the scent of greasy food and stale beer. He inhaled deeply, smiled, and looked across the small restaurant for Brian. He spied him sitting at a booth in the opposite corner, teasing one of the waitresses.

"Here he is," Brian said as Rob walked up, "what do you want to drink? I have been forcing this poor girl to sit here and entertain me while I waited for you."

"You better tip her well for that," Rob said then turned to the waitress, "No one should be subjected to that." He smiled. "I'll have a Bud draft."

"I'll be right back." The waitress said, and then walked off. Brian admired the view as she left, then turned back to Rob.

"So, who was on the phone?" Brian asked.

"Oh, Sarah. She's up at MacDill for her drill weekend. I guess we are going out to Channelside tonight."

"That didn't take long." Brian smirked.

"I know, but it should be fun."

"You know man, that girl has only been chasing you for about eight years."

"Yeah, well, I dunno. We'll see what happens. I have only been back for a few days. I want to keep my options open. Besides," He leaned in conspiratorially. "there is this chick upstairs from my new place that is stupid hot."

"Whoa big fella," Brian bellowed, "you know better than to shit where you sleep."

The server brought their beers over and set them in front of the two men. Rob turned to the woman, thanked her, and then brought his attention back to the conversation at hand. "It'll be fine, don't worry about it!" he said as he raised the beer to his lips.

Suddenly a blindingly white light spilled into the dark restaurant. It almost looked as if all the cars in the parking turned on their bright beams on at once. "What the hell—" Rob began to ask when the ground began to shake and a thunderous roar reverberated through the restaurant. Caught up in the cacophony, he did not even feel the cold beer splash into his lap. As the rumble died away, the light began to dim. Rob yanked up the dingy wooden venetian blinds to see the pillar of fire reaching into the sky from the southwest.

***

Smirking, Sarah flipped the lid of her cell phone closed and tucked it deeply into her hip pocket. Looking down, the outline of the phone could not be seen through the thick winter weight uniform fabric and she was content that her appearance was up to her stringent standards. Sarah Anderson had the reputation as a squared away airman, a reputation that she defended with fervor and therefore she ensured her person was squared away. This attention to detail or what some called just plain anal retentiveness had served her professional life for the last eight years.

"So who was that?" the olive skinned woman standing next to Sarah asked.

"Rob. He's a friend of mine from high school. Just got back into town and I want to, umm, catch up a bit." Sarah replied coyly.

"Is he cute?"

"Definitely -- in a tall, goofy, white-boy kind of way. But he and I have been playing this whole I like you when you don't like me game since high school. I figure he might be a fun rebound." She replied, grinning as she stood up and started to the door. The other woman followed closely.

"What brought this on? No, never mind, I don't care. At least you are not still hemming and hawing about Mike." the woman said, holding the steel framed door open for her shorter partner.

"Well Heather," Sarah said matter-of-factly," I had an epiphany."

"Ohh please," Heather cooed, "do tell."

Sarah looked up at the clear blue Florida sky and said, "I hate sleeping alone."

"Ahhhh." Heather responded, "And apparently Rob is a candidate to fill that void, huh?"

"Low hanging fruit, you know?" Sarah answered with a wry smile and continued walking toward the canary yellow Mustang convertible parked a few yards off. "With all seriousness, I have managed to keep in touch with him over the years and he is a pretty great guy." She continued in a conspiratorial tone. "So I will spend some time with him and decide whether or not to use my womanly wilds to convince him to 'fill that void.'" Both women laughed out loud as Sarah clicked the unlock button on the keyfob. The women simultaneously opened the car doors to let the built up heat from the beating summer sun out of the enclosed space. Even though the car had only been parked for forty-five minutes, the combination of the black canvas top and dark asphalt turned the inside of the vehicle into a blast furnace.

Sarah slid into the cracked leather bucket seat and started the car. A moment later when cool air began to hiss through the dash vents, Heather ducked into the car and both women slammed shut the doors. Reaching over the center console, Sarah flipped the climate control knob to 'Max Air' and buckled her seat belt. The drive back to BDOC was only about a mile across base, but being Security Forces meant she was acutely aware of the consequences of getting caught driving without wearing a seat belt. Besides, she really did enjoy driving versus walking the sprawling base. "I guess that rules out 'girls night' tonight?" Heather asked as she flipped down the visor to check her makeup.

"In a word… yes." Sarah responded curtly as she pulled out of the parking lot and smiled. "However should things not play out as planned, I *expect* you to answer your phone immediately so that we may continue the evening."

Heather scoffed, turned the visor up and responded flippantly, "Well my dear, I will be bristling with anticipation." Again, both women burst out into the giggles. She then hit the power button on the radio and the car's interior filled with an R&B song from the latest one-named artist. As they sung along in harmony, the car slowly snaked along the seemingly random twists and turns of the base roadway.

Just as the female singer was hitting the crescendo with the two ladies howling along, the Mustang pulled into a 'RESERVED' parking space in front of a large brick building. Through the hazy windshield of the vehicle, the Security Forces building cast a long shadow in the afternoon sun. The architecture suggested that the building was built in the late sixties with the only upgrade being several large antennae platforms that sprouted from the roof like metallic horns. A large wooden sign, clearly weathered by the harsh Florida climate, filled the grassy void between the parking lot and building. In contrast to the sign itself, the letters proclaiming '927th Security Forces Squadron' shone in a coat of fresh paint. An emblem, depicting a large schooner with raised masts and a KC-135 tanker, offset the lettering representing MacDill Air Force Base.

After parking the car, both women hastily exited the Mustang. Slamming the doors in concert and replacing their berets, the two began walking toward the tempered glass entrance doors. A flash of light to the north caught Sarah of guard from the corner of her eye. Quickly twisting sideways to admonish the brash camera person who photographed her without permission, she could see a bright yellow light that seemed to loom over downtown Tampa. Parting her lips unconsciously while taking in the scene, she began to ask, "What the he—".

A rolling thunder washed over the two women, drowning out the question on Sarah's lips and causing everything to thrum like taut strings. Sarah looked to Heather. The olive skin of her cheeks was streaked with tears and her face was a mask of horror. The rumbling subsided as a gentle breeze began to blow in the direction of the light. Quickly turning to the north, the realization of what had just happened hit Sarah just as small cloud connected to the ground by a thick tether rose into the sky.

***

"Jesus Christ!" Brian cried. "What the fuck was that?"

"I don't know man, but that sure as hell looks like a mushroom cloud to me. Holy shit…"

The reception on one of the televisions suddenly snapped back. For about ninety seconds, a flash screen displayed on the screen with the words, 'Emergency Report' emblazoned on a red and orange undulating background. The picture then cut to an obviously shaken brunette female anchor, hair muffed and suit jacket slightly askew, which had begun speaking. "We interrupt your regularly scheduled programming for a special report. Moments ago, a large explosion rocked the bay area. Initial reports are that the explosion was centered at Tampa International Airport. We are currently trying to contact both the airport and the Tampa Police Department for … wait," She put her hand to her ear, "I am told cell phone footage was just emailed to the station from outside the airport." The picture cut to a grainy and shaky video of a plume of smoke emanating from a large charred crater where the terminal building should have stood. The video panned to see airplanes tossed around the area like toys. Several buildings had collapsed, caught fire or both. The picture cut back to the anchor who had gone ghostly pale and looked on the verge of passing out. "Right now the cause of the explosion and whether it was conventional or possibly nuclear in origin is unknown. Tampa, St. Pete and all surrounding emergency response teams are reported to be en route to the area. Again, we do not know the cause of the blast, however the president was scheduled to make a stop in Tampa and meet with Governor Crist." She raised her hand again to her ear, "We have just had an unconfirmed report from one of the rescue teams that there is radioactivity detected at the blast site. This would seem to confirm," she hesitated, "erm, confirm that the blast is of a nuclear device."

Brian stood up and grabbed Rob by the arm. "Come on man, we are getting the hell out of here." They started walking towards the door and as they left, Rob could hear their waitress sobbing to herself in the corner. Brian hit the door locks and they both jumped in. Starting the car, he tore out of the parking lot back toward the office. The road was open, with cars pulled to the side. Passengers were collected outside in small groups observing the clouds. "Everyone still seems stunned," Brian said.

"Yeah," Rob said, pulling his cell phone out of his pocket, "we need to get back before all hell breaks loose. And I imagine it will not be long before it does." He hit the speed dial for his parents' house but got an operator saying all circuits were busy instead. "Shit!" He said, "Well, the cell phones are down."

"Figures," Brian said as he cut off a Prius to make a turn. The tires squealed as he accelerated down the street. A few moments later they pulled back into the parking lot of Brian's office. Tina ran out of the office toward the BMW. He turned to Rob, "You should come with us to the house. We have plenty of room and now isn't the time to be driving across town. It's gonna be a damn madhouse out there!"

"Thanks man, but I am going to try to make it to the apartment. I think this is going to get ugly real quick, and I want to get home where I have some supplies—," he was interrupted by Tina banging on Brian's window and screaming.

"Alright man," Brian said, "Get your ass home and be safe." He grabbed Rob's hand and shook it. "Gimme a call when this is all over and let me know you're ok."

"Will do." With that, Rob opened the door and got out. Tina bumped him out of the way, jumping in the car and hugging Brian.

Rob opened the Jeep door, getting and starting the engine. He turned the radio to the local news station and pulled out of the parking lot. He looked down briefly, hitting the redial on his phone. He prayed silently that the call would go through to his parents.

***

The sirens howled like banshees and rave lights flashing through the windshield are how Harris usually describes a ride in the cramped cab of an ambulance. The only distraction in the Spartan gray plastic interior was the scuffed control panel for the aforementioned lights and sirens. The radio was currently a cacophony of confused calls and questions from the various units being dispatched to the scene.

The breakdown of usual strict discipline and professionalism on the radio seemed to be centered on what exactly happened at the scene and what kind of dangers they were about to face. Harris was disconcerted that the usual calm, cool, collected emergency response personnel seemed to lose their bearings under the stress of the situation. Of course everyone was secretly worried sick about what they were getting themselves into, but no one was supposed to show it. The low rumble that shook the station, followed by the small vertical pillar with a mushroom top seemed to confirm that it had been a nuclear explosion. None of the powers that be had a confirmed cause so the call had come in as a catastrophic hazmat accident and that was exactly how it would be handled.

Davis was steering the truck through the vehicles seemingly abandoned at random on the thruway. "There's the HINT," he said pointing at a slightly larger vehicle that had parked at the service road that led into the airport. The HINT unit is a specially outfitted vehicle specifically designed to handle situations involving hazardous materials. Slowing as they approached the larger truck, one technician could be seen setting up a large orange tent lined with spray nozzles. Several aquamarine kiddie pools were laid out at intervals next to long handled brushes and pressurized cylinders with attached nozzles that looked like extermination equipment. Flanked on either side of the Hazmat truck were Tampa Police cruisers, which had been first on the scene. A trio of officers were taping off the quarantine area and setting out cones blocking all lanes in or out of the airport. In the sky above, the cloud that had been looming over the scene for the last 20 minutes had begun to disperse in the gentle breeze coming off Old Tampa Bay.

"Looks like they have the Decon station set up." Harris said as he switched off the sirens. The unit's tires crunched over the gravel on the shoulder and ground to a halt. The two men jumped out of the truck and headed over to the HINT unit. "Hey!" Harris said jogging over to the guy next to the large truck who was pulling a SCBA, self-contained breathing apparatus, over his shoulders.

The SCBA is not unlike the standard SCUBA tanks used by divers. They both use compressed air to provide an uninterrupted supply of breathable air to the wearer in hostile environments. The major difference is the SCBA mask is full coverage like a gas mask and maintains positive pressure to prevent the introduction of any outside contaminants. Used by most fire fighters, both civilian and military, they have become the standard in the industry.

"Are we still handling this like a standard Hazmat spill?" Harris called to the man near the HINT unit.

"As far as I know," the man answered. "The trucks are having a hell of a time getting through the traffic, so we're on our own until they get here." He threw the mask over his shoulder, causing the thick rubber hose to land on his shoulder with a muted jingle. "Fucking rush hour…" he muttered as he turned to Harris. "Look, we have to stay here and finish setting up the Decon area. Why don't you two head toward the post office." Then pointing to the crater where the main terminal once stood, "Because I hate to say it, but there isn't shit here."

"Roger." Harris said, turning and heading toward Davis who was helping to test the spray nozzles of the individual tanks. "Davis," he called, "we need to head over to the Post Office and see if there are any survivors."

Davis set the nozzle down, slapped the technician on the shoulder and said, "Good luck man," before walking quickly toward Harris. "What? We need to wait for the trucks," he managed to say before Harris cut him off.

"They are stuck in traffic. Apparently, it's going to be a while before they show up. Until then, HINT is in charge, and we're search and rescue." Harris replied as they jogged to the truck.

"You know, they have a whole team for that." Davis replied angrily as he opened the rear door. "This really blows. We're EMTs, we help people, not look for them."

"Dude, quit your whining. This is what all that training was for!" Harris exclaimed as he walked around the boxy side of the truck. Finding the handle he was looking for, he opened a panel exposing several GTFE suits and two SCBA pack. Slinging a pack over each shoulder and grabbing two protective suits in the crotch of his left arm, Harris snapped close the panel. Walking around to the back of the ambulance, he opened the right hand door with a click. Tossing in the suits and setting down each pack with a clang on the metal floor, Harris jumped into the back and slammed closed the door.

Turning over the engine, Davis turned and called, "Fucking dig it!" smirking as he placed the transmission into drive.

Davis' normally cast-iron stomach turned uneasily as he looked out on the devastation before him. It dawned on him that up until now, this had just been another call. For some reason he suddenly thought of kids. Just how many kids were in the airport when that happened? I bet they were excited to come to Florida and see Mickey. They had probably been looking forward to it for months… "Argh!" he yelled, slamming his hands on the steering wheel and then took a deep breath. Exhaling slowly, he compartmentalized his feelings once more as he turned the unit toward the wreckage where the Post Office had once stood. Blackened metal beams stood upright in the rubble like a fossilized rib cage protruding from cement rock. The twisted and charred remains of automobiles were strewn across the debris field, tossed around like children's toys.

Davis stopped the ambulance on the blasted cement drive that led to the Post Office.

"Davis, we need to do these screenings so we can get out there." Harris called from the back. Davis turned to maneuver his way into the back and was having a great deal of difficulty. The new ambulances had been touted as being much roomier and easier to move around in. He unfortunately was taller than most at 6 foot 3 inches tall, and this led him to smack an elbow or knee on every bulkhead or piece of equipment as he made his way to the rear.

"Damn!" he cursed, rounding the jump seat and in the process banging his knee on a rack holding several heavy duty flashlights. Harris was sitting on the gray vinyl covered bench directly across from the portable stretcher fiddling with the blue vital sign monitor. Davis flopped down onto the stretcher sending it bouncing off the closed cabinets in the bulkhead. Pulling up the short sleeve of the left arm, he slid on the blood pressure cuff. Harris clipped the pulse monitor onto his pointer finger, slid the probe into Davis' mouth and hit the cycle button. Several seconds later the machine let out a tinny beep.

"135 over 80, 65 bpm, pulse ox 98… not bad," Harris said sarcastically.

"No kidding." Davis deadpanned as he slipped off the cuff, tossing it at the other man and hitting him in the chest. Sliding on the cuff and clipping on the pulse monitor, Harris punched the cycle button a second time.

After a few moments, "127 over 75… eat it buddy!" he said with a smirk. After yanking the sleeve off and setting the meter aside, Harris grabbed one of the canary yellow SCBA packs. In order to don the SCBA, he first pulled an arm through both of the padded shoulder harness straps and snuggly fastened the waist strap. Next, he pulled the mesh covered rubber straps over his shaved head. Pulling the straps taunt to ensure a proper fit, he tested the seal. Finally, he opened the valve to start air flow to the regulator. Looking over to Davis, Harris flashed thumbs up as the other man finished adjusting his mask. After a moment of fidgeting with the harness to ensure a comfortable fit (or as comfortable as these damn things can get, he thought to himself), Davis flashed a thumbs up back.

Each man then grabbed the red rubberized HAZMAT suit. The suits were meant to protect the wearer from various hazardous chemicals and were outfitted with a large clear plastic viewing hole in the front of each suit. Sitting catty-corner to each other, they laid the suits face down and unzipped the backs. In the cramped space surrounded by various pieces of medical equipment, the two men clumsily stepped into the suits. After sliding on the red rubber gloves that accompanied the suit, they completed putting on the suits, each man zipping up the other's suit in turn. In their final act, each man wrapped the wrists of the suit in red duct tape to form an airtight seal. Harris looked back behind the bench seat to find the black mesh medical bag and lift it out of its place. Davis grabbed the black plastic backboard by its integral handles and in a muffled voice said, "Let's go." Harris nodded, grabbing the door handle and pushing the rear double doors open.

Davis' stomach squirmed again as he exited the ambulance. He didn't know why it was so unnerving from this perspective after seeing it all outside the windshield of the truck. Maybe, he thought to himself, it was the warehouses and industrial buildings, easily seen off to the north, partially obscured by a thin brown cloud. There should have been a large concrete and glass structure with thousands of people filling the void. Planes should have been coming and going, looking like large aluminum birds swooping in for their prey. The emptiness combined with the soundtrack of distant sirens provided a surreal soundtrack to the solemn view.

As Davis stood stupefied, Harris began to survey the rubble looking for any survivors. Yeah right, he scoffed sarcastically to himself; this definitely wasn't a nuclear bomb. His mind suddenly drifted to a documentary he had caught one day on some historical channel on satellite. A large cement building filled the screen, the roof looking as though a giant hand had ripped off its top. In the center of the rubble glowed a red molten mass. Helicopters and planes were dumping load after load of sand in an attempt to corral the radiation spewing forth from the disaster. His mind then cut to a scene of several rows of vehicles. These had been the first responders. The engine trucks, tanker trucks, ambulances, and construction equipment that was rushed to the scene to save people or property. Completely abandoned, looking serene but so irradiated that no human could safely approach it for years to come. The final horrific scene was that of an orphanage, filled with children with horrible birth defects from missing limbs to severe mental retardation. All caused by errant radiation.

Harris stopped dead in his tracks. His suit suddenly felt like a leotard collapsing in on his stout frame. Harris began to breathe fast and hard, flirting with hyperventilation as fear crept over him. Without thinking, he began to calm himself and his training taking over. He had only graduated about six months ago, and controlling his fight or flight instinct was something they had drilled into him. After several seconds, he was able to refocus. Once again, he closely scrutinized the disaster area as a blotch of color caught his eye several hundred yards away in the gray-black devastation. Some blue object, what exactly it was he could not make out, seemed to be swaying back and forth in the distance. Harris started carefully making his way through the debris field, trying to avoid any shards of shattered glass or exposed rebar that would pierce his suit. Reaching about half way to the object, he could now see that it was a person thrashing about in a pile of rubble.

"Oh my God!" Harris exclaimed, picking up the pace and quickly covering the distance. The man was in the center of some sort of building since an outline could easily be seen. The strange part was that this building seemed to have collapsed inward into what could have been a basement. What struck him as odd was that in Central Florida, especially this close to the bay, the water table is so high that it is virtually impossible to have a basement.

Harris ignored the odd feeling and began picking his way toward the figure that continued to flail wildly. Loud growls and groans replaced the distant sirens as the only sounds to be heard in the desolation. The body was facing away from him rocking back and forth almost keeping time. "Fire Rescue, we are here to help. Please calm down and we will try and get you out of there." Harris said so as not to spook the man. At the sound of his voice, the man seemed to thrash even more wildly. He could see that the man's legs were splayed out before him and covered in large pieces of cement. "Davis, can you hold him while I try to move some of this debris?" Harris asked, voice muffled by the facemask. When there was no response Harris turned to see Davis, about 150 years away, slowly making his way toward him. "Damn," he muttered under his breath then yelled, "Get over here I need some help!"

Davis picked up his pace slightly as Harris turned back toward the man.

Rounding the trapped man whose continued thrashing had yet to slow, Harris took a closer look. The blue he had seen in the distance was apparently some sort of HAZMAT which was now severely damaged. It didn't look like the same suits issued to first responders however. From the slashes in the suit, it was noticeable that the plastic was significantly thicker and less rubbery. Additionally, a tail like protrusion from the back looked like a hose connection to hook into an air supply. The suit itself was covered in blood that had leaked out of the battered man inside. The man continued growling in pain and reached out for Harris.

"Sir, calm down. I'm here to help, but I need you to relax," Harris called through his mask as he tried to look into the man's face. The transparent viewing port in the suit was bathed in a thin film of crimson from his trauma, but a long slit in the middle opened like a maw to show the man within. One good eye peered out from the left side of the face while the right side was a mass of shredded meat. The man growled and spit as he tried to reach for Harris. Shock, he thought to himself as he crouched onto his haunches. I need to get this guy out of here ASAP. He thrust his right arm out palm first and fingers spread like a cop signaling to stop, trying to get the man to lie back. "Sir, lie back, you are going," Harris was cut off as the man reached out and clamped an iron grip onto his forearm. Before he could react, he was pulled forward and in the same moment, the man rocked toward him. One heartbeat later, Harris' fingers broke the plane of the damaged suit.

Harris first felt an uncomfortable crushing sensation followed immediately by a searing pain that shot straight up to his shoulder. He began to howl as adrenaline dumped into his blood. Pure instinct took over as he pushed his stout frame back with his legs to escape the trap. The pain exploded once again into the damaged hand as the middle finger snapped. With a sick audible ripping, the flesh of the finger tore and separated. Harris let loose a blood curdling scream from the mixed horror and pain as he lost his balance and fell backward. Hitting the ground butt first, his head swung back to hit a broken piece of cement, losing consciousness, and thankfully winked out.

CHAPTER TWO

"We have confirmed reports that the blast was nuclear in origin," the radio reported as Rob tried again unsuccessfully to call his parents and threw the useless phone onto the passenger seat. "The Tampa police department is asking everyone not to leave their homes or places of business. This will allow rescue workers to arrive more quickly to the scene. Keep all doors and windows closed. Do not use the air conditioner, as it may bring contaminated air into your home. Rescue and decontamination teams are on the scene and are said to be bringing casualties to local hospitals as well as MacDill Air Force Base. The governor has asked that a state of emergency be declared, and the President is going to speak within minutes. The southeast region FEMA has been mobilized and is heading into the area. Department of Homeland Security is coordinating all efforts with local authorities…" He turned the radio down.

Well, he thought to himself, it wasn't a very big bomb, I guess. He leaned over and switched the air conditioning to recirculation. It was probably a terrorist trying to pick off the President. I always said a suitcase bomb would be the next 9/11. He grabbed his cell trying once again in vain to dial his parents. All circuits are busy, big surprise.

Rob was about half a mile from Brian's office when he ran into the first problem. A fender bender had the intersection blocked. Several cars were stopped in front and it was quickly threatening to become a traffic jam. Rob looked to the right and saw that the sidewalk was clear. Seizing the opportunity, he steered around the frantically honking traffic onto the vacant sidewalk and headed for the intersection. The accident was in the middle, which allowed Rob to weave in front of the waiting cross bound traffic and around the accident.

He heard a crash and looked back in time to see a dark blue sedan trying to follow his lead clip a black SUV that was inching its way across the intersection. Rob allowed himself a self-satisfied smirk and continued down the avenue toward downtown. Glancing to his right, he could see the interstate packed with cars heading north out of the city. At the moment, it appeared as though they weren't heading anywhere. All the traffic was at a standstill. Well, Rob thought to himself, at least downtown shouldn't be too bad.

Reaching the collection of overpasses and ramps that marked the beginning of the downtown he yelled, "Shit!" Through the windshield he could see the cars backed up on the entrance ramp that stretched out into his lane. Looking around he saw that the oncoming lane was full as well, waiting to get on the ramp. But, he noticed, that the off ramp was clear. There was a slight incline of grass that lead to the cement ramp and a chain link fence that marked the edge of the pavement. He thought that if he could get up that incline and over the fence, he could ride the off ramp past the traffic to the other side. Jaw set, he put the Jeep into low. The truck bounced and jumped as he drove up the curb, onto the center median. The traffic honked an angry song as he drove by and reached the incline. He sped up just as his tires hit the grass and the truck climbed its way up the incline. There was an echoed pop as the bumper connected with one of the posts supporting the fence, and a grating crunch as Rob drove over the fence onto the ramp. He started down the ramp, slowing momentarily to look at the indicator lights on his dash. He sighed in relief, no lights were lit, and therefore it appeared he had managed not to damage the mechanical workings of the truck. Dropping the truck back into drive, he drove down the ramp to the other side of the intersection.

Rob made his way through downtown, which appeared almost deserted. The occasional vehicle or flashing yellow intersections was the only hiccup along the way. The path remained clear until he reached Bayshore Boulevard which ran parallel to the bay. The road was packed in both directions with people trying to get out of south Tampa or apparently to get into MacDill. The bridge that would take Rob to the island that held his apartment seemed miles away. Surveying the clutter, Rob saw an opening to cut into the neighborhood that bordered the congested avenue. Edging slowly into the neighborhood with its cobblestone streets and plantation style houses, he followed other vehicles that were also trying to cut their way past the clogged artery. This path too came to a sudden end. Well, I guess I can hoof it, Rob thought, and took advantage of an open space in front of a large white colonial style house to park. Grabbing his keys, he pushed open the door and jumped out. Slamming the door shut and hitting the lock button, he headed down the block toward the overpass that would take him onto the island.

Rob easily made his way through the couple of blocks that lead to the bridge by weaving between cars, snickering at cat calls and ignoring complaints by the upset drivers stuck in traffic. Reaching the cobblestone lane that lead to the large cement overpass, he jumped back just as an ambulance screamed by him. Oh yeah, the hospital he thought to himself as he stepped back out onto the lane, crossing it to the right side to stay out of any other potential traffic. Suddenly the air was filled with the steady whump-whump-whump of the hospital helicopter approaching, no doubt bringing in more survivors. Making his way down the middle of the island toward his apartment was a bit unnerving. There was an eerie stillness that clung to the afternoon air. As he walked, he could see people loading up their vehicles here and there, but other than that, there appeared to be no motion at all. Usually the island would be alive with activity: cars passing by, young mothers out walking with their children, retirees out for their daily constitutional, but now there was no sign of them. He thought again of his parents, and reached into his pants to retrieve his cell phone. Smearing the screen with sweat from his fingers, he dialed. The same message replayed yet again, and he shoved the phone back into his pocket. Looking ahead, Rob estimated that he had about a half mile to go and decided to jog the remaining distance to try to clear his mind.

***

The small cabin buzzed with voices, each trying to speak louder than the last to be heard above the din. Larger than life faces loomed over the men and women of the room, their teleconferenced voices further adding to the cacophony. The small room had become stifling and the Chief of Staff called the stewards on the intercom to adjust the temperature of the room. Unfortunately, the heated caterwauling of the overly excited personnel kept the room sweltering. "Alright, enough!", ordered the short man at the front of the room, slamming his meaty palms upon the cream Formica tabletop.

Despite his short stature and bulldog-like features, the President of the United States was a commanding presence. The man's frame, while bulky, still retained the musculature from playing right wing at Boston College. This was due in part to his commitment to practice with his son David at a local Virginia rink. While his physical characteristics and the obvious fact he was President could be intimidating, the main reason for his authority was his attitude. While normally a jovial "everyman" from New England, when crossed, he tended to get extremely ugly. This was a holdover from his stint in the Army where he had what some thought, mostly his superiors, the distasteful habit of viscously berating soldiers under his command when they stepped out of line. This earned him the nickname of "Dirty Harry" among his commanders and also ensuring that he would not serve any longer than his first commitment. In his next endeavor into the pharmaceutical industry, the opposite was true. The attitude served him well, gaining recognition while relentlessly clawing his way up the corporate ladder and was looked upon kindly by senior management. Within an unheard of period of only seven years, "Dirty Harry" went from a lowly junior department head to Chief Executive Officer of Waylan Pharmacorp.

Seeming to have the world as his oyster after making his fortune at the ripe old age of 34, Harold "Harry" Maggio set his sights on politics. A series of politically motivated inquiries into the senator from his great state of New York provided the opening Harry was looking for. A bloody, mud-slinging campaign ensued with the troubled and embattled incumbent. By using will and wilds, he barely squeezed out a win with his moderate conservative platform. Once in office however, Maggio let his true conservative colors fly. He introduced bills for sweeping changes to the social reforms and tax increases of the last administration. Backed by the popular support of a right swinging public opinion, the bills were a success and Harry was seen as a rising star on the political stage. His popularity at a peak not only amongst his constituents but also the country as a whole, he threw in his hat for a presidential nomination. Although his popularity all but assured him the nod, a token primary was held and he won support in a landslide.

The presidential campaign was a knockdown, drag out, smear effort on both sides. Several of the men who were under his command while in the Army and employees that he had subverted to get ahead at Waylan PharmaCorp, all successfully spoke out publicly against him. For the first time, it was "Dirty Harry's" turn to be on a sharp decline with voters. It was only a piss poor judgment call by his opponent that saved his presidency. Reports that old Michael Griffen could not keep it in his pants and knocked up a campaign worker swarmed the networks. In response, the polls swung decisively in his favor. On that fateful day in November, Harry Maggio won the election.

An abrupt and complete hush had fallen over the room. The only sounds were the rumble of the immense jet engines and some feedback from one of the teleconference screens. To drive home the point, Harry reached over to the remote, turned off the volume and then threw it at the floor in disgust. Exhaling brusquely, he turned to face the mahogany wood paneled wall. Harry ran his fingers across his slowly expanding forehead (his kids called it a five head, yuk, yuk) through his thinning hair and arched his back to stretch. A satisfying crack accompanied the apex of the stretch and he breathed a relieved sigh. Slowly he unbuttoned the top button of his shirt and slid the tie off his neck. Turning he said, "Look everyone, we have been at this since the explosion happened and, pardon the expression, we still can't find our asses with both hands. So this is what we are going to do: we are going to take ten." Harry glanced at his watch and looked back out at the cluster of worried faces. "We will reconvene at 18:15 hours. In that time, I want you to stretch and get your thoughts together. Jim," he pointed to the director of Federal Emergency Management Agency, "get with Bobby. I want a status update on relief efforts. Dale, John and Ty, I want you to put your heads together and come up with the most likely groups responsible," he said nodding to the floating heads on the video screens, directors of various intelligence agencies. "Dick and Helen, I want you to discuss our military option. Everyone else, get your shit together as well by the time I get back." The president grabbed the door handle, pulled it open and stepped through toward his personal office. Christ, what a fucking mess, he thought to himself.

An unfortunate idiosyncrasy left over from his Army days, was the use of profanity during stressful situation. While cognizant of the uncouth tendency, it still sometimes got the better of him. Knock that shit off Harry, he said to himself and a thin lined smile briefly appeared on his lips as he stepped into the presidential office. In order to maintain a constant temperature, the window shades had been drawn down and the room was bathed in a soft glow from the recessed lights in the overhead. A pocket of cool air enveloped the president as he stepped into the room and closed the door. The low pile cream and tan star patterned carpet gave slightly as he walked around the large cherry desk to sit in the plush office chair. Harry had just sat down when a sharp knock broke his refuge. Ten minutes was too much to ask for, apparently. "Come in," he said facing the door as it swung open.

A tall man stepped into the room with a myriad of ribbons splashing color against a stark contrast to the metallic Chairman of the Joint Chiefs badge on the opposite side. Gold bands and three gold stars adorned the sleeves of the dark jacket. "Admiral, I thought I asked everyone to take ten?"

"Sir, I apologize," the Admiral interrupted, "but this cannot wait. There is a situation on the ground you need to be made aware of that will drastically change the way you handle this situation."

Harry's initial anger melted away and a gnawing feeling began in his gut. "What do you mean Admiral?"

"Sir, as you know in the time since the explosion I have been in contact with the Joint Chiefs to determine the readiness of our forces. During these correspondences, Admiral Mendelson notified me that contact has been lost with the Naval Medical Research Center Lab Oceanus in Tampa."

"We have reports of problems with communication throughout the area, Admiral," the President said impatiently, "both with hard lines, cellular and satellites, even at MacDill. They are probably just having the same issues."

"Sir," the Chairman said, "Oceanus was a special access program classified medical research project that was located underground on the Tampa International Airport site."

The President looked at him intently; his patience was beginning to grow thin. "Go on."

"Sir, I have the Director of the Naval Medical Research Center in Maryland, Captain Ashland and the Director of the CDC on teleconference. They can explain more thoroughly than I can."

The Admiral walked over to the door, cracking it to say a few words to the staffer outside, then quickly closed it again. On the large LCD display directly across from the president's desk, a shoulders-up view of two figures appeared on screen side by side.

"Thank you for your time Mr. President. I assure you this is of the utmost importance," the khaki clad man stated. A silver eagle and gold oak leaf flanked both sides of the man's collar below the surprisingly youthful face. "I will try to make this quick, Sir." Captain Ashland cleared his throat and began again. "As I am sure you have been informed, the Oceanus Lab was a Specialized Access Program located in Tampa." The faces on the screen flashed blank and were replaced by a computer generated overview of an airport. "During World War II the Army Air Force federalized Drew Field, what is now Tampa International Airport. During its use by the military, various improvements including munitions and personnel bunkers were built on the site. After the war, it was transferred back to the civilian municipality and remained relatively unchanged until the early 1970's when plans were laid for a new airport facility." The screen cut to black and white head shots of several men and women.

"At the same time, several prominent doctors, scientists and researchers left government research labs to establish a new school of Medicine and Bio-Medical research at the University. These were some of the best and brightest of the cold war warriors, and the consensus amongst many was that they were to be kept in the fold at any cost." The screen cut back to an aerial photo of the Tampa International Airport with labeled buildings and a red outline of a structure extending south below the Post Office. "The renovation of the airport gave a prime opportunity to build a secret, state-of-the-art research facility to be manned by top scientists, beneath the prying noses of the Soviets and the American Public." The screen dissolved back to the two figures.

The President looked down at his watch. Five minutes had passed and Harry, more irritated than before barked, "I understand that this facility has more than likely been destroyed by this incident and that billions of American tax dollars are gone. But if you are done with your history lesson, I have other..."

"Sir, you do not understand!" the director of the CDC blurted, a small mousy woman with dark hair and cat eye glasses. "That lab was a genetic engineering lab that worked with some of the world's most virulent and deadly viruses."

There was a moment of calm as the President bowed his head and rubbed his temples with the tips of his short fingers. Looking up, eyes filled with fury, Dirty Harry exploded. "So what the hell are you trying to tell me exactly? What the fuck were you were making down there? Has some goddamn superbug been released to the winds by that explosion?"

On the screen, the mousey woman cringed. She then actually jumped back from the camera as if she was going to be pulled through the screen and angrily slapped. The Captain simply set his jaw and began speaking again. "Mr. President, you are exactly right. We do not know what happened. That is why I asked the Admiral to allow us to brief you on the situation." Pulling a manila folder with "Top Secret – Special Access" stamped in red on the cover from off screen and placing it on the desk in front of him, the captain began to read as he spoke. "Sir, all the specifics of the project are not important. The lab was not developing biological weapons as *specifically* prohibited by the Geneva Convention." Squinting, he produced a pair of gold wire rimmed glasses from his right pocket and placed them on his long face. "Oceanus was primarily a medical research facility."

"Captain, skip the delivery and give me the baby." President Maggio said irritably.

"Sir, the bottom line is that we have a potential problem with the HTO virus." the Captain said as he quickly scanned the rest of the report before looking up. The gravity of the situation dropped over his face like a curtain as he continued. "The Human Terminal Operability Virus was supposed to be the next greatest advancement in battlefield medicine. Designed to be administered to fatally wounded soldiers on the battlefield, its goal was to allow the body to continue to function for up to 24 hours after the initial trauma. The virus would propagate in the bloodstream, resulting in almost instantaneous clotting. It would then move to the brain, blocking pain receptors and sharpening sense centers until the body simply collapsed. However, according to the reports there were some, uh, problems."

"Problems?" the President probed sarcastically.

"Yes sir," the Captain responded. "Unfortunately, all attempts thus far have failed to produce a viable candidate for field testing. At the current stage the virus has had unforeseen effects on test subjects." The captain hesitated for a moment, looking down before clearing his throat and looking back into the camera. A thin film of sweat could be seen clearly on his ample brow. "It seems upon injection into the test subjects the animals would promptly die. But sir, uh, I don't know how to say this, but the animals would reanimate and try to attack the researchers. In initial tests, one individual was infected by a bite from one of the test subjects. The young man died several hours later only to reanimate in the morgue and attack other personnel. The infection continued until security was finally able to destroy all the infected. In total, 30 people were infected and killed in the incident within one hour."

An unnatural chill filled the room, causing goose bumps to break out up and down the President's arms. A quiet knock on the door interrupted the silent reverie. "Mr. President," the soft voice of a female staffer could be heard through the door in the bulkhead, "everyone is standing by with your briefings."

"Just a minute!" the President turned to the door and roared. He took several deep breaths to calm himself then said, "I will be out in a few more minutes. Tell everyone to sit tight."

A frightened but muffled, "Yes sir," carried into the room as the staffer acknowledged his reply.

Turning back to the screen he asked, "What are we looking at here? How is the virus passed? What are the chances it survived the blast?"

"As far as transmission, from the data it is blood borne and can only be passed through bodily fluids. The threshold of survivability of the virus would depend on whether the virus was exposed to the atmosphere of the lab at the time of the explosion and then had an available host. Even in the unlikely event of an infection, the probability that the infected could dig their way through the rubble to endanger the public is extremely low." the Captain answered.

"Sir, if I may interject?" the mousey woman asked with authority, obviously recovering from her earlier shock. "I may be able to shed some more light on the situation."

"Please." Harry said, again running his hand through what was left of his hair.

"As the Captain has so eloquently put it, there would have to be an occurrence of perfectly timed events in order for an infection to even happen. However, I would like to dispatch an assessment team to the area immediately to report on the situation. Just to cover our bases." The woman unconsciously pushed the hair from the left lens of her glasses as she looked down in front of her. Speaking as she read, the director continued. "The team will study the situation on the ground and report back with any pertinent information. Additionally, they will advise officials on the ground as to the nature of the threat. Upon confirmation of infection, the team will begin inoculation of those in direct contact with those infected and direct containment."

"There's a vaccine?" the President asked, his eyes opening wider with a small glimmer of hope.

"Yes sir!" the woman promptly responded, "There is a vaccine. But unfortunately there is only a small stockpile of doses here in Atlanta. For sake of safety, we are going to coordinate to provide several doses to you and your staff when we are provided a location. In the meantime the team will bring enough vaccine to contain a potential outbreak and protect those who deal with the infected."

"I agree, let's get moving on this immediately." Harry said as he pushed himself up from his seat, nodded at the two figures on the screen and looked toward the bulkhead door.

"Mr. President," the Admiral said as he walked across the star covered cream carpeting to the oak desk. Quickly setting a black briefcase on the desk face, he snapped it open, pulling out a manila envelope sealed with a thick red adhesive band. "One more thing," he said placing the envelope in front of the President.

Harry noticed the dark look on the Joint Chiefs Chairman's face and his anger that had threatened to explode once more instantly cooled. Picking up the envelope and a letter opener from the desk, the President slit the red seal of the envelope. He opened the folder and began skimming the first page, then the next, and the next until after several strained moments he fell back into his chair. "Jesus Christ! Is this for real?" The President, his voice gravely and quiet, asked.

"Unfortunately it is, sir." The Admiral replied solemnly.

"Operation Nero… containment of uncontrollable contamination due to biological weapons…use of thermonuclear weapon only effective means of complete containment…" The President spoke as he read. "Potential cover scenarios…termination of military personnel involved in sanitation." Harry said shaking his head, looking up and throwing the open folder onto the desk. Getting up from his chair, Harry motioned for the Admiral to follow. "Let's not get ahead of ourselves here. Keep me updated on any word from the CDC. But this does not leave this office, understand?" Harry asked as they reached the door.

"Yes sir." the Admiral replied as he walked through the open door.

CHAPTER THREE

By the time Rob reached his apartment, he was drenched. Unlocking the door, he stepped into the house and was greeted by the welcoming hum of the wall air conditioning unit. He closed the door then loosened his slimy wet tie. That finished, he unbuttoned his sweat stained shirt and pulled it over his head. He pushed the power button on the television and looked toward the air conditioner. The warning from the radio came to mind as he started toward the unit. Pulling off the plastic cover over the blower, he removed the air filter and glanced at the writing on the cardboard frame. "Allergen Reducing H.E.P.A. Air Filter," could clearly be seen in red lettering. Sighing with relief, he fitted the filter back into unit and replaced the plastic guard. He remembered that they had used HEPA filters on the sub to prevent any radioactive particles from contaminating the ship. Smiling, he turned the air conditioner up to its highest setting and made his way to the bedroom. As he threw his moist shirt in a pile of dirty clothes and began pulling off his pants, he could hear the voice of the President from the other room.

"…vicious and unprovoked attack will not go unpunished. I know the hopes and prayers of the nation are with the people of the Tampa Bay area. I have declared a State of Emergency in the affected area: FEMA, the Department of Homeland Security, the National Guard and local law enforcement have all been mobilized in the area to aid in the rescue efforts and maintain order. All air, rail and naval traffic have been suspended and a no fly zone is in effect over the entire Tampa Bay area. I ask that in this time of crisis, we help our neighbors and help authorities to do their jobs through cooperation and teamwork. God bless you and God bless the United States of America."

As Rob pulled on his jeans, he heard the station cut to the local anchor, "The President addressing the nation as we find out more about the explosion. As he stated, The Department of Homeland Security and FEMA are coordinating their efforts with the Tampa Police and Fire Departments in order to quarantine the blast area, maintain order and help those hurt in the explosion. We have been receiving reports that local hospitals are being overrun with people concerned over radiation exposure, making it difficult to deal with actual casualties. FEMA asks that unless you have an injury requiring medical assistance or have been directly exposed to the blast that you remain in your homes. They state that this was a very small bomb with very little fallout and that teams are evacuating residents in areas that will be exposed to the greatest danger of radiation. Otherwise, please stay in your home with the air conditioner off …"

The television became muffled as Rob bent down to reach under his bed. Pushing aside pile of dirty running clothes, he fumbled under the bed to grab a large gun case. Hard plastic brushed at the tips of his fingers and he pushed the case in a bit further before catching hold. Rob could feel the strain of the stretch as he pulled the black case out and pushed the blanket aside to set the case on top the bed. Leaning over, he grabbed the soggy slacks, pulled out the slick key ring and unlocked the gun case. Inside, lay a Barretta 9mm and a Winchester 12 gauge pump shotgun. Both weapons were well cared for and gleamed dully from a recent oiling as sunlight fell through the windows. Picking up a magazine for the pistol,

Rob took several moments to inspect the rounds. Once satisfied, he grabbed the 9mm and slid the clip in with an audible click. Several movements followed in quick succession: pulling the slide back, releasing it to chamber round, and engaging the safety. Setting the readied handgun down onto the foam interior of the case, Rob then grabbed a box of 3" magnum shells. After pulling out six shells, he picked up the shotgun and with a flick of his wrist turned it over the shotgun. The smooth wooden stock felt good in his hands as he slid six shells into the magazine, checked the safety and set the gun back onto the bed. Okay, he thought to himself, that's done. Next we need some clothes. Reaching over and grabbing a t-shirt from off the floor, Rob gave is a quick smell. There was the faintest musk of sweat, but after looking around for a better option, he decided that it was passable and pulled it on over his head. Upon getting up, the news was droning the same information as before in the other room.

He sat down next to the case on his bed, resting a moment, and started to finally process everything that was happening. Nuclear bombs, martial law probably, heh, so much for the new job. Hell, he might even end up getting called back to active duty just to help clean up the mess. He reached over to his night stand to grab his cell phone in an attempt to try his parents one more time. Looking at the screen just prior to punching the speed dial, he noticed a chat request in his messenger program. Navigating to the icon to start chat, Rob saw that the request was from Sarah. How am I getting cell service for the damn messenger but not the phone, he thought. A small WiFi symbol on glowed in a soft blue on the corner of his screen and the realization that the phone had connected to the home network sunk in. It made sense, he rationalized. The computer networks were generally hard wired, redundant systems and more than likely would still work. If the phones aren't out at their house I can just use Skype to call. Hopefully I can bypass some of the congested telephone switches and get a call through.

"Hey, you there?" Rob typed into the messenger. He sat waiting for a minute and received no response. Sliding the phone into his pocket to wait for the inevitable vibration when he got a response, he went to the fridge to grab a soda. Just as the door snapped closed, the phone began to vibrate. He quickly walked over to the television to mute the sound and sat down at his computer desk while pulling out his phone.

"Yes, are you ok?" She had typed back.

"Yeah, I am fine. I was over off Nebraska and Bearss when it happened." he replied. "I hauled ass back home before the traffic got too bad. How bad is it there?"

"I am fine. They have us escorting the ambulances as they come in and trying to keep everything under control."

"Good to hear."

"I gotta go, I just wanted to make sure u were ok. Take care of yourself."

"Sure, and be careful… we are supposed to go out tonight :)" he typed, smirking.

"Yeah right, you too. Bye" The message flashed and the screen showed she had left the chat. Well, at least someone is ok, he thought. Setting the cell phone down, he grabbed his Internet phone and dialed his parents' number. There were several clicks and one ring before an error message stating that the call could not be completed.

"Damn it!" he said out loud. Then he had an idea. His parents were always having computer problems and Rob had put a remote access program on their computer so he could access it whenever they did. He pulled up his browser and attempted to log into their computer. After several seconds, the screen said "connecting" and suddenly he could see his parent's computer desktop. The browser was open and the website of a local newspaper was pulled up. It was on a comment section for a news story about the local hospitals. A message all in caps caught his eye as he moved the curser to the two way chat icon on his screen.

"I AM AT GENERAL HOSPITAL AND STRANGE THINGS ARE HAPPENING TO THE PEOPLE COMING FROM THE EXPLOSION AREA. I AM IN THE ER AND WE HAVE PATIENTS COMING IN WHO SEEM TO BE DOA, OR DIE WHEN THEY GET HERE. BUT THEY START TO MOVE AROUND AGAIN IF LEFT ALONE! THEY HAVE EVEN GRABBED AND BIT PEOPLE. RADIATION CAN'T DO THAT."

Bull, he thought to himself and then was interrupted as the page changed. He quickly clicked on the chat button and a white window filled half the screen.

***

Davis had hastily applied a pressure bandage to Harris' wounded hand at the scene and despite the excruciating pain; the two had managed to strap the crazed victim onto a backboard for transit. The injured man, bloodied and broken, had continued to wildly thrash and attempt to bite at Harris on the hurried trip to the ER.

At first the truck had been routed to the Catholic hospital just a few miles to the northeast. Unfortunately, backups clogged the main arteries that fed the interstate and blocked their way. They had since been rerouted to the general hospital across town. Despite the incessant howling of the sirens and flashing lights, the truck only made a grudging pace through the heavy traffic. In the interim, Harris attempted to stop the bleeding in his hand. Despite the direct pressure on the wound that made his nerves sing, the blood continued to seep through the pressure bandage. Every piece of gauze and every bandage that Harris used was soaked in a matter of minutes. By the time the ambulance pulled under the emergency entrance, the floor of the truck was covered in bloody bandages and a large crimson flower had bloomed on the front of Harris' shirt.

The back doors swung open without warning sending bright sunlight into the back of the truck, stunning the weakened EMT. "Jesus," a nurse murmured taking in the crazed scene. A broken man, thrashing and growling wildly on a portable gurney and a bloodied EMT staring at her with vacant eyes seemed to fit in with the surrealism of the day thus far. "Let's get the gurney first," Davis said struggling with the nurse to get the collapsible stretcher out of the high vehicle. Before he had a chance to warn her, the crazed man caught hold of the flesh of the woman's bare forearm. She squealed as large red gashes formed on the golden tanned skin. A young man dressed in turquoise scrubs came running out of the glass double doors at the sound of the scream, wrenching the claws away and pinning the injured man to the stretcher.

Davis turned his attention back to Harris who was swaying unsteadily as he attempted to step out of the ambulance. "Whoa buddy!" he cried as he took hold of the man's arm, gently guiding him to the cement below.

"I'm ssokay," Harris slurred holding his injured arm to his chest. This was the first time Davis had seen the amount of blood his partner had lost.

"Christ," Davis mumbled, then said in a soothing voice, "I got you buddy, let's get you some help." The clogged road ways and distance from the scene showed in the near vacant state of the emergency room. A couple homeless people who looked like they were attempting to get out of the blazing summer heat by requesting superfluous medical treatment, roamed aimlessly through the waiting room. Davis guided the unsteady Harris to the intake desk. "Harris, Jason." he said to the nurse behind the counter. "He was attacked by that patient we just brought in who bit off his pointer finger."

Harris attempted to slur out a sentence, "Ihhhhhhhvvvlstaaaablld,"

A loud screech of static burst from the radio on Davis' hip as a call requesting his status echoed in the empty room.

"It's okay, I've got him." the heavyset intake nurse said as she guided Harris down into a waiting wheel chair. "Just let your dispatcher know where he is. We will coordinate with them after he's stabilized."

"Thank you so much!" Davis replied hurriedly, relieved his partner was now in good hands. Leaning down, he spoke to the injured man, "Hey buddy, they're going to patch you up, alright? You'll be fine. I'll come back to check on you when things settle down." Harris started another slurred reply when the nurse turned the chair to speed him into triage.

Since arriving, a stream of doctors, nurses and hospital personnel had looked at Harris' injury. While they had managed to stop the bleeding by suturing the wound, the infection had spread like wildfire up his arm. In the interim, angry red lines had begun radiating from his bandaged wrist up the arm to the shoulder and his uniform was drenched in a cold sweat.

Harris seemed to chase after consciousness, trying desperately to prevent lucidity from slipping away. Adrenaline flooded his system, sharpening his focus as a blood curdling scream echoed from beyond the small curtain divider. When this was followed by the metallic crash of stainless steel instruments spilling onto the tile, he leapt off the exam table. The color seemed to drain out of the world only to be replaced by a dingy grey tunnel. Swaying to the left and stumbling through the thin curtain, Harris came to rest against a structural pillar. As the world swam back into focus, the bomb victim they had brought in was perched atop the nurse he had met earlier. Grabbing the woman's lower leg in a vice-like grip, he sunk his teeth deep into her flesh. The resultant spray of arterial blood painted a macabre scene on the flat white wall. As Harris turned, he heard a wet ripping as the flesh was ripped from the young woman's lower extremity.

Choking on his gorge, he pinballed his way down the corridor, past the excited co-workers who were rushing to help the screaming nurse. The sounds of the screams muted slightly as Harris continued stumbling along, making several turns at random. "Wherethehellam…" the EMT tried to think through the fog in his brain when he was suddenly overcome by uncontrollable shivering. The shaking intensified, sending Harris toppling against a teak-colored door. His legs began to give out from beneath him, as his good elbow accidentally caught the horizontal door handle causing the door to swing open under his weight. Two stumbling steps later, the man collapsed onto the floor and curled up into a fetal position, shaking violently. Harris' last act was to let loose a strangled cry from the cold tile floor as his muscles convulsed for the last time.

***

"Dad, are you and Mom ok?" Rob typed.

"Yes! Thank God you're alright! Your mother and I have been trying to get a hold of you for the last two hours!" his father typed.

"I know, the phones are overloaded I guess. But at least the Internet is still working."

"How far away from the blast were you? Have you been contaminated? You have to come out here. Your mother and I are leaving as soon as possible but the roads north are all parking lots."

"I know Dad. I saw I-275 on my way back home. I was over by Temple Terrace when it happened. I am fine but I don't think I will be able to get there any time soon. I even had to leave my truck on the other side of the bridge and walk to my apartment." He paused for a second, and then typed. "Hey Dad, you still have your Luger?"

"Yes, and I am way ahead of you Rob. I already have it out and loaded. I imagine this might get a whole lot worse before it gets better."

"I know, people are animals, but I am glad to hear it. Listen Dad, I am going to stick it out in the house here. Keep your instant messenger on so we can talk. I have the messenger on my phone up so you will be able to get a hold of me."

"Sure, that's a good idea. Do you have enough food? How about water?"

"Yeah, I have plenty of food Dad and a bunch of bottled water, too. I am also gonna fill the tub up just to be sure. But listen Dad, I am glad y'all are safe. Tell Mom I love her and I will talk to her later. Love you."

"Love you too Son." With that, Rob clicked out of the remote control software and hit the home icon on his browser. The homepage was dominated by an aerial photo of large crater in what looked like a field surrounded by industrial buildings. It took him a sec, but then he recognized what used to be Tampa International Airport. South of the crater, he could see a sink hole that looked to have swallowed a couple buildings. Must have been caused by the shockwave, he thought. The forums link to the right of the picture caught his attention, and he decided to see what everyone had to say and what the damage was like first hand. Scrolling through the list of different topics, the page was filled with frantic cries of concern: radiation fallout, missing loved ones and topics about God's wrath. Rob noticed a strange post:

Title: THIS IS GOING TO SOUND CRAZY BUT CAN RADIATION MAKE PEOPLE MOVE AFTER THEY DIE?

Post: I am not crazy. I work at the University Hospital, and they have been bringing in people steadily since the explosion. We wanted to save everyone, but many were too far gone when they got here. The morgue is full and we had to leave body bags in the chapel. I happened by the chapel and looked in, and some of the bags were moving! I was horrified that we had put live people in the bags. I grabbed an orderly to help me check it out, and he unzipped the bag. The body lurched at him and bit his arm, taking some skin with it. The body growled and started thrashing. We both ran out of the chapel screaming and locked the doors from the outside. There are more growls and thumps coming from the chapel, and we have decided that the patients coming in take priority. Has this happened anywhere else?

Rob stared at the screen. He listened to the air conditioner hum and click as he thought about what he had just read. Weird, that is the second time that has popped up, he thought, and from two different hospitals. He grabbed his phone, and clicked to open his messenger. "Hey, you have a sec?" He typed, sending the message to Sarah. Setting the phone down to wait for a response, Rob walked over and surveyed the living room for the television remote. Aha, he thought to himself, there it is. Perched on the far end of the forest green overstuffed couch was the remote. The events of the day had already worn Rob out, but fortunately the desire to unmute the television overcame his desire to sit on his ass. Standing up, he walked over to the remote and flipped the sound back. Then the tall man half jumped, half sat down on the couch, throwing his feet up on the arm that until just moments ago held the remote control. As had been the case for most of the afternoon, the local newscaster was repeating emergency procedures, warning people to turn off their air conditioners, etc. Rob changed over to one of the cable news networks to see if there was anything different. He recognized the middle aged reporter; he was the one who always made snide comments while talking about the latest scandal or political maneuver. He looked harried today and was talking to another reporter on the phone.

"… from our affiliate in Tampa via satellite phone. How are things down there David?" The man on screen asked.

The slight muffled voice on the satellite connection started, "Shep, it seems things are going as smoothly as can be expected. I am here in Land O Lakes, which is just north of the Hillsborough County border, where Tampa is located. The National Guard has blocked off the southbound lanes, but has been very helpful controlling traffic that has been trying to leave. They have been stopping every vehicle to do a quick once over with a Geiger counter to check for radiation, a small inconvenience considering everyone has been advised to stay in their homes. Additionally, anyone who has attempted to get any further into Tampa via the southbound lanes, including us, has been stopped and not allowed to enter the Tampa area."

"Have you spoken to anyone that has been evacuating and if so what do they have to say?"

"We have, we have. The general consensus is that while there was extensive damage to the airport which we have all seen pictures of, there wasn't much collateral damage done to Tampa or the bay area in general. People's biggest concerns right now seem to be radiation from the blast and the fallout."

"Yeah, that seems to be on everyone's mind when there is a nuclear explosion." he said snidely. "What about relief efforts? Have you seen FEMA or the Red Cross since you've been there?"

"There is a FEMA relief station set up in a field here near the interstate off ramp, which has been aiding anyone who seems to need medical attention or decontamination. I did see a Red Cross vehicle try to get past the road block, but after a heated discussion with some soldiers, it joined FEMA off the interstate. Shep, I have to tell you that we have driven the length of Interstate 75 this afternoon, and as of an hour ago, every exit into Tampa has been blocked. Only traffic leaving Tampa has been allowed to exit."

"Well thank you David," Shep said, "and we will continue to talk to you as this crisis continues in the Tampa Bay Area. " The camera changed angles, and he looked into the camera. "The big question everyone is asking is how did this happen? How did a nuclear device enter the United States without being intercepted…"

***

Chad pushed through the solid oak doors that led into the office of the Director of the Centers for Disease Control. The large room was sparsely decorated; the walls were covered with bookcases full of medical tomes, civic awards from various non-profit organizations and framed copies of several degrees from institutions of higher learning. A lone and sickly looking fichus tree stood limply in a far corner. Two rather Spartan-looking brown leather chairs sat opposite the desk. The small woman seated behind the large desk looked like a cherub as she was bathed in the light of the late Atlanta afternoon. Despite the diminutive physical presence, Chad had felt the quiet anger on more than one occasion. Her bite was most definitely worse than her bark. Wasn't it Roosevelt who said, "Speak softly and carry a big stick?" he thought to himself. Well, that was definitely the case with Director Fuller.

The mousey woman was typing intently while staring at a large LCD monitor, looking up only when Chad had made it halfway across the large office. Director Fuller pushed a button on her phone and the quiet was filled with the abrupt female voice that answered. "Yes Madam Director?" Since the blast, everyone had been on edge, and it was starting to show at the edges.

Helen Fuller dismissed the tone and replied curtly, "I am unavailable until the end of this meeting. No interruptions."

"Yes ma'am" the voice replied. Director Fuller lifted her finger, looking toward the man before her. Slightly disheveled, she thought to herself that seemed to be Leske's general state of being. His dark blue blazer had several long creases from where it had apparently been sat upon, the paisley tie had been loosened at the neck, and drops of sweat could be seen bleeding through the shirt at the neckline. His shabby appearance alone would have been enough to stop him several rungs below his current position had it not been for his strict attention to detail in his work. This, combined with the ability to keep his mouth shut as her sounding board, meant that he would follow on her coat tails wherever she went. Currently, he held the position as Assistant to the Director of the Centers for Disease Control.

Clearing her throat she said, "Leske, good, please give me a status update."

"Yes ma'am," he replied confidently, "I have the team assembled: Myself, Dr. Rosenfelds, Dr. Maryweather, and several technicians. I have notified the flight crew and the Gulfstream will be fueled and ready upon our arrival. The containment, treatment and quarantine equipment has been requisitioned and is already on its way to the jet."

"And the vaccine?" Director Fuller questioned.

Lifting up the stainless steel briefcase and setting it on the oak desktop, Chad opened the case. The felt lined interior did not look much different from your standard briefcase with pouches for notebooks, folders as well as slide-in pen holders. Despite the otherwise pedestrian interior, a small clear box with a large biohazard label was snuggly wedged in the bottom of the case. Several clear vials and hypodermic needles stood out through the clear case. "I have the current working vaccine right here ma'am. But Madam Director, if I am not mistaken isn't this only about 50 percent effective at preventing infection and even then--"

"Leske, let me ask you a question." the director asked sternly, narrowing her eyes and staring intently at Chad. "Would you prefer zero percent effective?"

Chad could see he had to tread very carefully, gulped and stammered, "No ma'am. I am just concerned about its effectiveness on the ground. What if it mutates?"

"That is what Operation Nero prevents Leske!" she said strongly. At the mention of Nero, the man's eyes became saucers and he crouched over as if punched. The Director softened her tone. "Look, the statistical probability that the virus has been exposed to atmosphere alone is astronomical, let alone the possibility there was a human nearby to infect. This will be nothing but a quick trip just to ensure there are no potential outliers. You will be back in D.C. before you know it. Just take the team down there, shake hands, kiss babies and report back immediately once you get a sense of the situation."

Chad straightened up slightly at the confidence shown by the Director. She's right, he thought. The team will just take a look around, inoculate a few key players while down there and be back for the Redskins game on Sunday. "Yes ma'am, thank you ma'am." He replied softly, nodding. While snapping closed the suitcase and lifting it off the desk, Chad said, "I will be in touch with you once we are wheels down at MacDill."

"Very good," she said cheerfully, "and Godspeed." Chad turned to walk to the office door. As he strode away, Director Fuller turned her full attention back to her computer screen. Before Leske's interruption, she had been looking through the jumble of news coming out of the Tampa area. Refreshing the page and reading down the page, one story caught her eye. It was a very rough piece on local hospitals obviously posted in haste to beat other networks to the punch. But what had peaked the Director's interest was the comment section posted directly below the story. The topic line read, "CAN RADIATION BRING DEAD PEOPLE BACK TO LIFE?!"

CHAPTER FOUR

A sudden knocking at the front door distracted Rob from the television. Getting up, he muted the television again, and set down the remote as he made his way to the door. Looking out the peephole, a fisheye view of an attractive brunette filled his vision. Tiffany from upstairs, he thought to himself and then laughed. I guess it's the end of the world, I wonder if I am the last man on earth. He laughed to himself again and after regaining his composure he opened the door. The grin still hung stupidly on his face. "Hey Tiffany, how are you doing through all this?"

"Rob, I am really scared. I am sorry, but I saw you come home and my roommate's not home," she said hurriedly, "and I can't get her on her cell and I didn't to be alone."

"Hey, no problem, come on in! We can sit and watch the same news over and over together." he said as he winked at her. This seemed to relax the young woman slightly as she walked past him and plopped down onto the couch.

"What's going to happen?" Tiffany started again, the anxiety still in her voice. "I don't know anything about radiation poisoning. They keep saying on the TV just to stay indoors and we will be fine. But I don't know..."

"Look," Rob interrupted, "We will be fine inside. Hell, even outside we would be okay. It was a very small bomb and..."

It was her turn to interrupt, "How do you know?" she snapped. Rob raised an eyebrow at the terse question and shut the door with a quick flick of his wrist. He walked over to her, sat on the arm of the couch, and leaned over toward her to look her directly in her blue eyes.

"Remember last night when I told you I was in the Navy?" he asked in a measured voice.

Tiffany looked at him defensively, "Yes, why?"

"Listen. My job was to work on nuclear reactors. We had to learn all about radiation, what it can do to you and how much it takes to hurt you."

She looked up at him with her eyes suddenly full hope. "So okay, are we going to be okay?" she asked.

"Ok, like I said it was a small bomb. You saw on TV how small the crater was, right?" She nodded her agreement. "Alright, so if that was a big bomb, the crater would have been at least a mile across. I figure it was a suitcase bomb that some terrorist bought from somebody in Russia or something. But that's not the point; the point is that because it was so small there won't be that much radiation given off. It'll be bad right by the airport, but we should be fine this far away. And all the stuff kicked up into the air will take a while to settle. But again, there won't be much 'cause the bomb was small."

She paused to think this over for a second and then asked, "But the radiation is still in the air, right, we still have to worry about the fallout?"

He put a hand on her shoulder and answered, "Like I said, there won't be much fallout 'cause the bomb was so small. But, I doubt that the fallout will even hit us. I bet it will blow right out into the Atlantic. So I wouldn't worry about it, okay?"

Looking up at him, she half smiled, "Thank you Mr. Nuclear Guy for figuring this all out and making me sound like an idiot."

"Nahh, I don't think you are an idiot. Maybe a poor and helpless woman… but not an idiot." he said smirking and once again winked her direction.

"Oh thanks, asshole" Tiffany said as she slapped his arm playfully and Rob thought he caught her sizing him up with her eyes. Suddenly, there was a buzzing noise from across the room, and Rob jumped up and crossed the living room to grab the phone off his desk.

"I have to be real quick," Sarah sent, "the wounded are rioting. We got called to hospital. PPL R attacking the staff."

"Aww, hell!" Rob said out loud. He hurriedly typed, "Are you ok?"

"What's the matter?" Tiffany asked with concern in her voice and turned to look at Rob.

"My friend Sarah is Security Forces over at MacDill. She says the injured are rioting." he said distractedly, still staring at the phone.

"Oh, wow." Tiffany replied, sounding suddenly distant and finding something interesting in the other corner of the room.

"I am ok. But we already have shots fired. They've got the hospital locked down." Sarah answered.

"Hey be careful!" he typed, "It is happening at University and General too. Keep me informed and let me know you're ok."

"U too! General is right next to you, Be CAREFUL!" She sent back and signed out of chat.

***

"Mike One-Zero to BDOC, in route" Heather spoke into the radio as she hooked the mic onto her uniform. She looked over at Sarah who had just slid her cell phone back into her front ABU pocket. "You ready for this?" the olive skinned woman asked as a steeled look of determination played across her face.

"As ready as I'll ever be," the other woman responded as she pulled out her 'Oh Shit' weapon. The M9, basically mil-spec version Berretta M9FS, was a bit of a running joke with the security forces. In general, an airman in

Security Forces would be issued both an M9 and an M4 rifle. The joke was that if the enemy got inside the range of the rifle (which they never should, ha, ha) 'OH SHIT, grab the M9!' This kind of humor pervaded the dark cop mentality of the Security Forces. Pulling back the slide, Sarah ensured a round was chambered and slid the weapon back into the holster for the short ride to the hospital.

Setting her jaw, Sarah began to psych herself up for the potential conflict. Deep breaths, she thought to herself, slowing her breathing and calming her mind. You've trained for this for years, finally time to earn that government cheese. She curled her lip up slightly at the thought, but a small twinge of fear still nagged at the corner of her mind. Unlike the rest of the flight, she had not deployed to the Middle East last year. She was slotted to go, but due to missing a period two weeks prior and subsequent positive pregnancy test quickly changed her plans. Not only did this cause her to miss a deployment, but her miscarriage after five and a half months led to the rift between Mike and her…

The harried chatter on the radio between BDOC and other units as well as incoming ambulances and civil authorities filled the cab of the SUV, shook Sarah out of her reverie. She could see the wildly flashing lights of several ambulances illuminating the hospital as Heather turned the Blazer onto Bayshore. Closing the distance, the two women could see that a perimeter had been formed in a semicircle at the hospital's entrance. A barricade had been hastily constructed of several vehicles and medical equipment with a large battlefield triage center set up behind. Medical personnel were ferrying back and forth between casualty victims, attending to their various injuries.

Heather pulled the SUV onto the grass next to the parking lot then turned to Sarah and said, "Let's go!" Both women slipped out of the Blazer, drew their weapons and headed toward the barricade. Two men in ABU's had their side arms drawn and aimed at the double sliding doors of the hospital. Sprinting ahead, Sarah reached the first man crouched behind a dark blue sedan. In the lights of the emergency vehicles the subdued parallel bars of a captain could be seen on the officer's collar.

"Sir," Sarah called over the triage bedlam, "what's the situation?"

"The casualties started rioting. The best I can make out that some of the victims, who I guess they thought were dead, weren't. They started making a raucous and by the time it got out of hand, the group had grown to about 25 with even more people starting to join in. The hospital went into lockdown and we were waiting for Security Forces to show up." the Captain responded.

"Sir, are there any hostages?"

"No, they are just rioting and attacking people at random. Hell, one of the bastards bit me too when I tried to help a woman who fell on the floor." the Captain answered, twisting his forearm to show an oval ring of teeth marks that had just broke the skin.

Heather heard the tail end of the Captain's story as she caught up with Sarah and spoke briefly into the radio mic. Sarah could not make out the tinny reply over the background noise. "Sir," Heather called, "other units are on the way." She turned to Sarah. "Chief has directed us to try and clear the entrance to the hospital until the other units arrive. Fast and low."

"Copy." Sarah responded nodding and stepped around the Captain to the end of the long sedan's fender. Lifting her right hand, she waved at Heather to follow and they sprinted to the front doors in a crouch. The frosted glass obscured the view of the hospital lobby, but a large dark figure could be seen moving inside. Sarah, followed closely behind by Heather, slowly moved toward the doors with guns drawn. The infrared motion sensor on the automatic doors detected the movement, causing the door to slide open with an almost inaudible whoosh.

The interior of the lobby was a complete disaster. Chairs had been upturned and pushed to all corners of the spacious lobby. Newspapers, magazines and various medical paperwork was scattered throughout, covering the shiny black and white checked nylon tile floor. Scanning the area directly in her line of sight, Sarah called, "Clear!" and the two women stalked slowly through the automatic doors. Heather quickly scanned right while Sarah looked left. "Clear left," she called.

"Clear right," Heather replied and moved to fall back in line behind Sarah. They methodically made their way clockwise around the large lobby, looking for any obvious threats. Reaching the nurse's station, the duo heard a low grunting and shuffling. Crouching low and rounding the side of the desk, neither woman was prepared for what they saw. A little girl dressed in a flowered pink sundress sat aside a bearded middle aged man in blue scrubs. The girl's pale legs from knees to ankles were gently splashing in a pool of thick dark blood while her head bobbled up and down over the fallen man's chest. Sarah's stomach did a summersault as the little girl raised up her head which was covered in clotting blood from chin to nose. Heather let out a startled gasp, causing the little one to swing her attention toward the two women. Letting out a garbled growl through a thick mouthful of blood, the girl slipped clumsily in the spreading pool as she scrambled toward the two women.

"Stop right there honey!" Sarah cried to the girl as her feet caught purchase on the slick floor. The only reaction was another growl, louder this time as most of the contents of the girls mouth were expelled, and sprinted to cover the distance between them. "I said stop!" Sarah again yelled, aiming the barrel of the pistol at her center of mass. The girl was about four feet away when Sarah made the decision that later she thought probably saved her life. Twisting sideways on the pad of her left foot, she shot the right leg straight out catching the approaching threat just off center in the chest. The powerful kick spun the girl around and propelled her against the back wall, leaving a bloody outline on the cream paint.

"Damn Sarah! She's just a little girl," Heather cried as she quickly made her way to the crumpled little body.

"Heather be careful, she's not all there, little girl or not." Sarah said in a guarded tone.

Heather bent down to roll the small, unresponsive body over and checked her Coratid artery for a pulse.

"Jesus Christ, she's dead!" she had just gotten out before the little girl sat up snarling and bite down on the dusky woman's ear. Yanking her head up, Heather left her earlobe in the little girl's mouth. "Awwwww Fuck, Fuck, Fuck!" she screamed, lifting her right hand, unconsciously pressing both her hand and gun to her ear. With her prey distracted, the girl latched onto the leg of Heather's ABU's and bit deeply into the fabric on her thigh. The airman let out another howl of pain and Sarah rushed to pull the sick girl off. Grabbing her by the nape of the neck, Sarah pulled her off and ripped out a large piece of Heather's ABU in the process. Small streams of blood could be seen through the torn fabric as Heather stumbled away from the thrashing youngster. Spitting out the piece of fabric, the girl let loose a blood curdling screech and Sarah threw her against the outside wall of the lobby with a sick thud.

Sneaking a brief look at Heather, Sarah asked, "Are you okay?"

"The little shit. Oww, yeah, I will live. Keep an eye on her. Shoot the bitch if she tries to attack again." Heather replied as she inspected her wounded leg. The shoulder of her ABU's was slick with blood. A distorted call came through Heather's radio, just as the doors to the exam rooms burst open. Several bloody figures, uniformed and civilian alike skid into the lobby. Locking the two airmen in their sights, they growled in unison and ran jabbering toward the women. Sarah put two in the chest of a khaki clad teenager and it took her a stunned moment to realize that it had not put him down.

CHAPTER FIVE

The realization that in fact General hospital *was* right down the street from his house finally occurred to Rob. Tossing his phone down on the desk and walking to the back of the apartment, he heard the television's volume turn back up as he stepped into the bedroom. "…reports of injured people rioting at local hospitals. Tampa Police and FEMA just released a joint statement that all local hospitals are reporting unrest. They request that unless it is a life threatening emergency, people stay in their homes until tomorrow morning. This will give authorities that are already stretched to the limit, time to resolve the problems at local hospitals…"

Rob looked out the bedroom window and suddenly felt very exposed to whatever was happening at the hospitals being so close. He pulled the cord and the vertical blinds fell to the window sill with a loud clunk. "What are you doing in there?" Tiffany called from the living room.

"Hey! Do me a favor and close all the blinds in the front room, will ya?" he replied.

"Alright, but get out here. There's more stuff about the hospitals on the TV." She said as she began to move around the living room. A series of muffled thumps followed her movements. Rob peeked around to the second bedroom to verify that the blinds were already closed before opening the closet door and reaching up to the top shelf. After feeling around for a few moments, he felt the nylon straps and pulled down a tactical leg holster. He then walked over and closed the open gun case with a snap. Grabbing it by the handle, he walked out into the living room, and set the case on the kitchen table. Tiffany walked up to Rob as he centered the case on the table and opened it once again. She gasped and took a step back.

"What the hell do you need those for?!" she almost yelled, giving Rob a distrustful look as she took another step back.

Rob sighed and turned to face Tiffany. "Look," he said plaintively, "I have now read two stories, heard a news story and talked to somebody at an actual hospital all saying that people are losing it and attacking people at the hospitals." He looked at her a bit sternly now, "And you know what? I feel like an idiot because it took me until a few minutes ago to realize that we are only about a mile from one of those hospitals!" He took a step forward now. "You ever heard the old Boy Scout motto of 'Be Prepared'? Well I plan on following it. Don't worry, I hope I don't ever have to actually use these," he pointed to the weapons, "but I will be damned if I am gonna sit here and twiddle my thumbs!"

Tiffany looked at him sheepishly and asked, "Do you think you will really have to use those?" She said the last word with disgust. "I mean, the police will handle it won't they?"

"Yeah, sure, in a perfect world, but in a perfect world nuclear bombs don't just explode at airports either." Rob took a breath to calm down. Getting excited wasn't going to help anyone. He softened his tone again. "I am probably just being paranoid." he said, "But I am just making sure that I can protect us if anything crazy happens, okay? I'll even show you how to use them if it would make you feel better."

Her face softened and she took a step toward him. "No, that's okay. I just overreacted. I'm sorry. I'm just so scared." She reached up on her tip toes and gave him a quick peck. "Thank you for looking out for me."

Rob smiled and said with a cheesy western drawl, "Awww shucks ma'am, ain't nothin'." He tipped the brim of a fake hat at her, causing her to giggle and walked back into his bedroom. After again reaching the closet, he grabbed a green nylon backpack from the corner. On a set of shelves in the corner he picked up a multi-tool in a black case and a large silver Maglite. Opening the bag, Rob tossed in the items and then walked down the hall and into the kitchen. Grabbing several bottles of water out of the fridge, he put them into the bag along with a handful of energy bars from the closet to round out his stash. Walking out of the kitchen, Rob made his way over to the table. Picking up the extra boxes of ammunition and putting them in the bag, he then set it down next to the table.

Tiffany looked up at him as he sat down near her on the couch. Rob relaxed and leaned back into the cushions. A muted grumble sounded from Rob's stomach, and the thought about eating ran through his mind for the first time since the bomb. "Hungry?" Tiffany asked and smiled. "Me too. What do you have to eat?"

Rob shrugged, "Heh. Well, I've got pizza, cereal, energy bars, instant noodles and beer."

"Guy food. How about I put a pizza in the oven?"

"You don't have to do that, you're the guest—"

Tiffany got up and said, "No, you relax. I want to feel useful anyway."

"Well, if you insist, I guess I will let ya cook me dinner." he said sarcastically. "Pizza's in the freezer."

As she walked in front of him, his eyes followed her bottom as she made her way toward the kitchen. Tiffany for her part, pretended not to notice. How, even in the midst of a nuclear disaster, Rob thought, can a man drop everything and focus on ass? It must be nature, or something. Shifting his attention back to the TV, he found the remote and switched the channel back to the twenty-four hour news channel. This time he recognized the anchor as the investigative journalist woman that is always trying to solve the newest news mysteries. She was talking to someone on the telephone.

Turning the volume up, Rob recognized the voice of the telephone reporter he had heard earlier in the day. "What is the latest from on the ground there Dave?" she asked the air.

"Well, things have gotten much worse. It seems as of approximately an hour ago that the National Guard is no longer allowing anyone out of the Tampa Area. As you can imagine, this has caused tempers to flare, and there have been several altercations between the public and the Military."

"Have you been able to talk to the Military commanders? Why are they not allowing people to leave?"

"I have not been able to speak with the officer in charge of this checkpoint and none of the soldiers we have spoken to will tell us anything other than that it is their orders."

"Dave, tell me about these altercations. Has there been anyone hurt? Arrested? What are they doing with the people once they stop them?"

"From what I have seen, there have been no injuries from these confrontations. They are simply telling people to return to their homes.

The soldiers are directing traffic through the median and back onto the interstate toward Tampa."

"Thank you for the report. We will keep checking in with you as the story further unfolds." She again looked into the camera, "That was David Rodgers from our local affiliate in Tampa. This news as well as the rioting at the local hospitals raises some troubling questions. With us now is our military correspondent, retired Navy captain James Everette." The camera pulled out to show a large man with close-cropped hair and a dark blue suit sitting next to the female reporter. "Captain Everette, from your experience can you shed some light onto why the military is stopping people from leaving the Tampa area?"

"Gretta, while I don't have the specifics as to why it seems a quarantine has been placed around Tampa, I can give you a few ideas. It seems to me that while we know that there was a radiological attack in Tampa, there may have also been a biological or chemical attack as well. Some nerve and biological agents may cause disorientation and agitation to exposed individuals when they attack the nervous system. This is only my opinion, but I think it is likely that there was a secondary attack of an unknown origin and the quarantine is in place to prevent the spread of the agent. I would have liked to ask the reporter you spoke to earlier if any of the soldiers were wearing any sort of protective gear or gas masks when dealing with the public."

"Do you really think there was a second attack?" the reporter asked with a concerned look on her face.

"It would certainly fit the worst case scenario. But again, this is only speculation on my part."

"Of course, captain. Thank you for your time."

"My pleasure." The camera panned left and zoomed in, centering the reporter on the screen.

Rob muted the television and looked around the corner into the kitchen. Tiffany looked at him doe-eyed and was obviously shaken. He cursed to himself for having the volume up so high. "I am sure we are fine." She blanched and he jumped up, catching her just as she began to sway. He half guided, half carried her over to the couch and gently sat her down. He looked into her eyes, hoping to calm her back down. "If we had caught anything, we would be showing symptoms by now. We will be fine here." Rob leaned down and gave her a peck on the forehead. "We're just going to relax, eat some frozen pizza and have a beer. Everything is going to be fine." She reached out to him, grabbing him and with surprising strength she pulled him into a tight embrace.

"Thank you so much." she spoke softly into his ear. "I don't know what I would have done without you." He could feel the warmth of her body as she pressed against him.

"Well, I did have plans tonight, but those seem to have fallen through," Rob said as the timer on the oven went off with a high-pitched beep and he gently removed himself from her grip. He flashed a smile at Tiffany then headed toward the kitchen.

After pulling the pizza out of the oven, Rob cut it and slid two pieces each onto paper plates. He then pulled two beers from the fridge and twisted off their tops. Precariously carrying a plate and beer in each hand, he made his way into the living room. Handing Tiffany her pizza and beer, he set his food down and walked over to the stereo. Selecting the "CD" option and pressing play, "Layla" played from the speakers.

"I hope you like Clapton." he stated, sitting down and beginning to eat.

"Is that who sings it? I love this song." she said with renewed vigor. The color was back in her cheeks and it looked as though the combination of food and beer were doing her some good.

They sat in silence eating their meal and listening to the music. When they had both finished, Rob grabbed the plates and empty bottles, tossing the refuse and opening two more beers from the fridge. Rob returned to the living room with the drinks, handing one to Tiffany while he took a long pull from his own. Glancing at his watch, he noticed it was almost ten o'clock. "Wow," he said, "time sure flies when you're having fun." Rob moved to the opposite end of the couch, sitting down and making himself comfortable.

"Is that what you call this?" she asked with a coy smile.

"I suppose it could be *more* fun, but it hasn't been bad so far. The company is a bit mediocre, but other than that, sure." Rob winked and a smirk played across his face.

"Oh sure, at least you aren't hanging out with some crazed ex-military type who is planning his own personal Alamo." Tiffany retorted.

"You make an excellent point. That person might actually be useful!" he said as he chuckled.

Tiffany feigned indignation, set her beer down and leapt into Rob's lap. "Is this useful?" She placed her lips on his and they parted as she kissed him deeply. Rob responded in kind and ran his arms the length of her lean, lithe body. Feeling his body respond, he shifted her closer into his lap.

***

"BDOC to Mike One-Zero, status report" Tech Sergeant Dillingham spat into the mic, after pushing the junior airman out of the way. Disgusted, he threw the microphone aside and grabbed the sides of the airman's office chair. Looking directly into the young woman's face and speaking in a low commanding voice he asked, "When was the last time you heard from One-Zero?"

Airman Martinez had not met as terrifying an authority figure as Technical Sergeant

Dillingham since boot camp. At just over six feet tall and built like a linebacker for the Saints, his soft, deliberate southern cadence was enough to terrify her.

"Sir, Mike One-Zero checked in thirty five minutes ago. I have been so busy coordinating the augmentees that I haven't gotten to checking in with them."

The large man welled up and paused. Clenching and opening his fists as he exhaled, Dillingham then spoke to the young woman. "You are relieved Airman." Turning to look at the pale young man working on an after action report at the next desk he said, "Staff Sergeant Jones, take over for Martinez."

"Yes sir." the Staff Sergeant replied smartly.

Looking up, multiple views of the entire base played on a bank of monitors. Images of rioters, military and civilian alike, filled roughly half the screens. The base had been locked down in Force Protection Condition Delta for roughly an hour with deadly force authorized and augmentee personnel called in. Still, the crowds were growing in size.

A cutting voice from the back of the room pulled Dillingham's attention from the bedlam in front of him. "Sergeant Dillingham, status report!"

Spinning around Dillingham stood erect and responded to his commanding officer. "Sir, we have additional mobile units as well as activated Augmentee forces combating and containing the riots. Unfortunately, at least one of the units mobilized to the hospital has lost communication with BDOC." Dillingham paused, and then continued. "Sir, request permission to take a patrol unit and assess the situation."

The Major took a moment to think it over and then replied, "It would useful to get eyes on the ground intel instead of these damn monitors. You are not to engage unless you are in eminent danger, understand? You are needed back here. Take one of the Blazers and I expect a report in 20 minutes. CENTCOM and SOCOM are locked down and the base CO expecting a briefing in 30. The last thing I need is one of my Flight Chiefs playing Rambo. We need to figure a resolution on the double."

"Yes sir!" Dillingham replied, walking across the large command center to the outside corridor. The sounds of BDOC started to fade as he headed toward the armory. The last garbled voice echoing down the hall was a report about rioters in body armor. Awww hell, he thought, I better make this quick. He made quick work of checking out the weapon including an inspection of the M4 rifle and signing the weapon out in the log. Dillingham then jogged out the side door a waiting patrol SUV.

Getting into the driver's seat, his right leg began to ache. Dillingham rubbed unconsciously at the healed wound, while his mind momentarily focused on the memory of the injury. He had been a minor deity at his high school and helping the Hornets to their first ranked High School National Championship team. This was the only route available to the poor west Tennessee farm boy to go to college and throngs of recruiters clamored to sign the rising star. Deciding not go too far from the family homestead, Dillingham signed a letter of intent to attend the University of Tennessee in Knoxville. The freshman showed true leadership and became captain of the top ten-ranked defensive squad. All that ended in his first SEC championship game as a viscous block from a Bulldog fullback ended his career.

The nationwide audience witnessed on instant replay the shinbone snapping and poking through the distended skin of the young man's lower leg. While the resultant injury would heal with several surgeries and physical therapy, Dillingham's mental state was shattered. Falling into a deep depression, he stopped attending classes and eventually was placed on academic probation. At the end of the semester he returned home to help on the family farm. The sullen young man even began contemplating suicide to end the perceived pain of his existence when an Air Force Recruiter approached him one day at the local feed store. The idea of helping his country for the greater good lit a spark inside the man. For the first time in what felt like years, he again had a purpose. After a few waivers he was sworn in and on a plane to Lackland Air Force Base. Dillingham has never questioned the decision in his ten years of dedicated service.

Sitting up and placing the vehicle in reverse, he pulled out of the parking space. The dark night lit up in a flood of colored lights as the SUV drove on the perimeter road around the distressed facility. Approaching the front gate, an ambulance was being waved away, the guards refusing to lower the cement barricades to let the emergency vehicle in. Outstanding, he thought, slowly continuing to scout the situation. Just as he passed the commissary, several civilians were rapidly heading toward the flashing lights of his patrol vehicle. Several even picked up speed to intercept the SUV, stepping off the curb and into the street. Dillingham accelerated to avoid the rioters and was momentarily distracted by their efforts. A sudden loud bump to his left sent his stomach plummeting. Slamming on the brakes and throwing open the door, he rushed to attend to the injured person.

Behind the idling Blazer, the twisted body of a middle-aged man in ABUs and wearing the rank of Colonel reached up toward the horrified Sergeant. "Sweet Jesus," Dillingham exclaimed and bent down toward the man. Blood soaked the right side of the uniform, blotting out the officer's name. "Sir, are you alright? You came outta nowhere." The fallen man began to struggle. "Sir, don't you move. I'll call for help." Turning around to get the radio from the cab, several figures could be seen swiftly covering the distance to the Blazer in the headlights. Dillingham hastily abandoned the radio and took up his rifle. "Halt! Don't come any closer!" he yelled and menacingly waved the rifle at the adversaries. Their only response was a chorus a guttural growl and howls. "DON'T COME ANY CLOSER! I WILL FIRE!" the Sergeant bellowed, chambering a round and taking aim. Squeezing the trigger resulted in a short report and sent the first person, clad in a jeans and a US NAVY t-shirt, falling to ground. A small flower blossomed on the man's chest. Bouncing off the cracked asphalt and pushing himself up, the man regained his momentum toward the Blazer. "What the..." Dillingham mumbled as he put another round in the jean clad man. This time the man spun like a top and flopped onto the ground, the round taking off the top of his skull. The other hostiles were closing as sharp tug from behind threatened to pull Dillingham off balance. Turning around, the Colonel was grabbing his leg and had the cuff of his pants in his mouth. "Sir!" he yelled, kicking violently at the officer on the ground. The Colonel held on with a firm grip attempting another biting assault as the Sergeant leveled the rifle at his skull.

CHAPTER SIX

Rob began working his hands under the bottom hem of Tiffany's t-shirt. Suddenly over the reggae beat of "I shot the sheriff" he could hear vibration of the cell phone, notifying him of a message from Sarah. Tiffany began grinding her hips into his when Rob pulled back. "Shit! Hang on."

She immediately sat back and went rigid. "You have got to be fucking kidding me?" She slid off his hips as she spoke.

Rob sighed and was about to chastise her for being a bitch but decided against it. I think enough damage has been done, he thought. Reaching the phone, he picked it up and read the screen. His blood went cold and a shiver ran up his spine. The display simply said, "HELP!" Quickly, he quickly typed a response.

"What can I do? What is happening?"

A moment passed, then, "Thank God you are there! The hospital is overrun. The wounded are attacking everyone they see."

It was Tiffany's turn to see Rob blanch and forgetting the earlier slight asked, "What is it?"

"Hold on." he said while frantically typing. "What do you need me to do?" He then responded to Tiffany, "I don't know. Sarah is in trouble. She says that the base is being attacked by the wounded and she needs help."

The phone buzzed, "I don't know. I am hiding and you are the only one I can ask for help."

"Don't you have your gun? Where are the rest of the Security Forces?"

"We were overrun at the hospital. Tried to regroup and were overrun again. I am out of ammo. PLEASE, I NEED YOUR HELP! CAN'T GET NOWHERE WITHOUT GETTING ATTACKED!! DAMMIT HELP ME!!" Rob cursed quietly under his breath. Inside, he was being pulled in separate directions. The relative safety and security of his home was very appealing. Unfortunately, this would involve leaving his friend who was frantically asking for help to fend for herself.

The other option was making his way several miles south to a military base, somehow getting onto said base, and then hunting down Sarah while people were rioting. The phone vibrated again, "PLEASE HELP ME!!"

"Ok – Where are you?"

"A utility shack at the southeast end of the runway."

"How am I supposed to get on base?"

"I don't know. I think it has spread all over base. There is no chatter on the radio. There's probably no one there."

"Alright. I am going to lose you until I get on base and get a signal back. I'll let you know when I am there. Just stay where you are." What the hell am I doing he thought as he typed on the tiny keypad.

"Thank you! Please hurry and be careful!" The small screen then notified him that she had ended the conversation.

Rob turned and looked at Tiffany who was staring at him with concern. Fortunately for Rob, it looked as though she had forgotten about his transgression from just a few minutes ago. "What's wrong," she asked, "You look terrible." An answer, however, eluded him. Am I really going to try to break onto a military base and save Sarah from a mob of homicidal people? He shook his head, trying to clear the fog that suddenly seemed to fill his skull. Resolve and determination took root in his mind. Yes.

Looking to the concerned woman on the couch, "Sarah is trapped on MacDill. It sounds like all that stuff we have heard about the people rioting at the hospitals is true and now they're attacking everyone."

"What? That doesn't make any sense. Don't they have like military police that can handle that kind of stuff?"

"Yeah, and she is one of them. But she says they have been attacked too, she's out of ammo and no one can help her."

"So what are you going to do about it?"

"Good question." he said as he turned away. Sighing, "I am going to go get her."

"You have got to be kidding!"

"No, I'm not. I am the only one who can get to her." Then Rob turned, "I'll walk you upstairs. It's a long hike to my Jeep."

"And sit in my apartment all alone? No way, I am coming with you."

"No. I appreciate the sentiment, but I can't ask you to—"

"You aren't *asking* me to do anything," Tiffany interrupted, "you expect me to sit here all by myself while all hell breaks loose out there? No way. Besides," she pulled out a set of keys, "I have a car. And since you don't have yours, you seem to be hating it right now."

The air was still while Rob momentarily thought of a response. She had a point about the car, but he couldn't bring her along. It is going to be dangerous enough as it is without having to look out for her. On the other hand, he could show her how to use the shotgun and have someone watching his back. He looked at her with stern resolve. "Fine, but you need to know a few things. First," Rob grabbed the keys out of her hand, "I drive. Secondly, I am going to show you how to use this shotgun."

Tiffany stood up and gave a little salute. "Yes sir!"

The shotgun lay in the open case on the table, gleaming in the overhead light. Rob turned, picked up the gun, and then Tiffany. The gun was cold in his hands as he held it out to demonstrate. "This," he pointed to the button in front of the trigger, "is the safety. Red means dead. Also, don't ever point it at anything you don't want to kill." He turned the gun over. "This is where you slide the shells in to reload, brass side back." Rob handed the gun to Tiffany, and he helped her steady it against her shoulder. "This is going to kick. The first time will probably catch you off guard. After that you will know what to expect. After each shot, you slide this back." He pointed to the slide that she held in her left hand. "This is to eject the old cartridge and chamber a new one. That's it. I want you to keep it out of sight unless we are in danger. Guns make people nervous, especially the police."

Tiffany looked nervous but firm in her resolve. Rob grabbed the tactical holster, wrapped the nylon straps around his thigh, and fastened them firmly in place. Picking up the Berretta, he checked to ensure a round was chambered, double checked the safety and slid it into the holster. He then grabbed the backpack and pulled one of the straps over his shoulder. Walking over to the door he opened it and said, "Let's go."

A small courtyard stood between the apartment and row of cars parked out front. As they passed through, Cabbage palms and other small shrubs tugged at their clothes. The parking area was nearly empty, with only three cars inhabiting the several spaces. Rob fingered the remote in his hand and looked across the parking lot to see which car the button unlocked. The lights on a green Volvo station wagon flashed twice and there was an audible click as the doors unlocked.

"That's my car." Tiffany said, driving home the message by pointing to the car Rob had just unlocked.

Walking over to the car, Rob slid into the driver's side and Tiffany followed suit on the passenger's. Twisting the key in the ignition, the car quietly turned over. He was about to put it in gear when some howling banshee of a woman, screaming along to a driving techno beat, spewed from the car's speakers. Lunging forward, he punched the radio off and looked at

Tiffany. "You can actually listen to *that*?" he asked incredulously. She just shrugged and turned the radio back on, switching to the local AM talk radio station. The radio announcer's voice sounded harried and Rob listened as he pulled out of the parking spot.

"I know we just put this out a few minutes ago folks, but I think with what we are hearing about what is going on out there we need to repeat this. The Department of Homeland Security is urging all citizens of the Tampa metropolitan area to stay away from all hospitals even if you are severely injured. They report severe civil unrest at all of the local hospitals, and state that until the unrest has been controlled by the military and local law enforcement, it is not safe to bring wounded to these facilities. FEMA medical stations are to be set up throughout the city, and we will report those locations when they become available. Additionally, DHS has stated that the area surrounding the Tampa International Airport has been evacuated and radiation surveys have been done. According to these initial surveys, the yield of the weapon was very low and initial radioactive contamination did not spread further than one mile from the blast site. They also state that fallout should not be an issue as the prevailing winds should take it directly out over the Atlantic by morning. A bit of good news everyone, you can turn your air conditioners back on! I want to go back to the phones here, we have Janet in Seminole Heights. Hello Janet, what can you tell us from Seminole Heights?"

Rob pulled onto the main boulevard to head off the island. The streets were deserted, but most of the houses had one or two lights on, looking like distorted jack-o-lanterns. Passing through the business district featuring a few small restaurants and shops, only one lonely bar was open. The door was propped open, and Rob could see two solitary patrons sitting at the bar. Driving further toward the mainland, only one person could be seen on the streets. In his passing glance, he could tell the guy was disheveled. Wearing the baby blue scrubs and white tennis shoes, he could make out the telltale uniform of a hospital employee. Rob could see dark splotches on the front of the man's shirt that looked like blood. I guess they don't change when it's this busy, he thought to himself. The radio droned on adding an eerie soundtrack to the quiet night.

"So what, umm, let me get this straight," the announcer said, "you work at the University Hospital and you… just left? I know they say there is 'civil unrest' but that doesn't mean you can just leave. Didn't you say you were a doctor?"

"I didn't say what I was," the female caller said, "I just said I got the hell out of there. I don't care what they call it, 'civil unrest' or whatever. All I know is the people that they brought in who died in the hospital got up and started attacking people."

"Come on!" The announcer said, "You are making this up, Janet. Maybe it was the families or friends of the people that died. Maybe they don't think the doctors did enough to save them. Are there a lot of police or military at the hospital? Are they making things worse? I know these are tense times, maybe they pushed some buttons—"

The caller interrupted, "I don't care what you *think* happened. I was there, I saw what happened. The bodies got up from the floor and started attacking people. Biting, grabbing, scratching, all trying to get at everyone who was in their path! And it's not just the people who got hurt in the initial bomb. A paramedic who had been working, like we all had, since it all began this afternoon, collapsed from exhaustion. Before we could do more than get him on a gurney, his heart quit and we couldn't resuscitate him. His body was in an exam room waiting to be brought to the morgue."

"That's a sad story, Janet, but we need to move on."

"No, listen damn it! There was a police officer, he was working security in the ER, and he was standing just outside the door of the exam room. Suddenly, the paramedic grabbed the cop's arm from behind and bit him on the arm. He latched on digging in his teeth, growling and shaking his head like a dog with a chew toy. The cop howled and whirled around, kicking the paramedic in the chest. He let go and crumpled to the floor in a heap. As I ran up with some gauze for the cop's arm, the paramedic growled and got up again. I ducked behind the cop as he pulled out his gun and yelled a warning for the guy to stop. He came at the police officer and the cop shot him in the leg. The guy only stopped for a moment, swaying, and kept coming forward. Another yelled warning and two more shots in the guy's chest, and the guy still kept coming. It wasn't until the cop shot him in the head that the guy stopped."

"Thank you Janet. Wow, okay, I thought enough horror had happened tonight," the announcer said with disdain, "but we have to move on. Mike in South Tampa, how are things in our neighborhood?"

"Oh my God," Tiffany said pleadingly, looking at Rob, "is that what's happening at MacDill? Is that what we are getting ourselves into? Shouldn't we let the police and the military handle this? I know she's your friend but if this is happening all over, how are we even going to get there?"

Rob locked up the brakes, and they were both thrown forward in their restraints. The butt of the shotgun smacked loudly against the dash as it slipped from Tiffany's fingers. "Fine!" Rob said throwing the car into park and grabbing the door handle. "My car is just over the bridge. I can walk from here." He grabbed the door handle and pulled. Nothing happened, and he tried throwing his shoulder into the door to force it open. Looking down he noticed, two things: his door was locked and he still had his seatbelt on. Taking a deep breath and looking straight ahead, he said calmly, "I told you I didn't want to bring you out here for this. I promised her I would help her, and I figured it would be dangerous. That is why I wanted you to stay back at your apartment."

"Why is it so important that you go out and save her? Why can't she wait for help from the military? I mean she *is* on a military base." She then looked at him intently, "Why does it have to be you?"

"Because she is more than my friend, she's like family." He looked at her, "I went through some stuff that I really don't want to talk about back before I went into the service. She was there. Sarah always listened and helped me when I needed her. I owe her for that if at nothing else. Now," he unlocked the door and opened it, "I can walk from here. You go back to the apartment where you will be safe."

"No. I'm sorry, I understand. I want to help."

"Are you sure? Once we get to the truck, I am not going to stop because you get cold feet. It would probably be better for you to go back."

"Like I told you, I don't want to be alone in my apartment. I would do some good. Besides, you need someone to cover your six…isn't that what they say in the military?"

"Something like that." Rob said as he closed the driver's door and put the car back into drive. He pulled away, beginning to cover the last few blocks before the bridge to the mainland. The announcer's excited voice interrupted their conversation.

"You are sure that you saw explosions coming from on base?"

"I said I heard explosions coming from MacDill."

"And how do you know they were explosions?"

"Look, I did two tours in Afghanistan, I know what an explosion sounds like. And those were definitely small explosives. But that was only in the last hour or so I was hearing gunshots for a couple hours before that. Must be what the DHS keeps talking about at the hospitals. But the gunshots and explosions sounded like they were real close to the front fence around the base."

"Thanks Mike. If anybody else out there has heard anything like that, please give us a call. I hope this isn't a second incident like the attack at the airport."

Rob and Tiffany stared at the radio, transfixed by what they heard. What the hell were they getting themselves into? They could almost hear each other think. Rob was starting to have second thoughts when Tiffany screamed. He looked up just in time to see a pair of headlights, looking like snake eyes, bearing down on the car. From the passenger side, the crunching of metal and the shattering of glass pierced the night air. They were both thrown forward, Tiffany hitting her head on the top of the door as it bent in the frame, and jerked violently back as the Volvo was driven into the bridge's guardrail. Rob's head snapped back, connecting with the driver's side window with a crack, and the world disappeared into inky blackness.

CHAPTER SEVEN

The day was bright with the Florida sun reflecting off the small waves in the crystal clear water of the swimming pool. The small radio sat on the white plastic table that played the newest Offspring album at an obnoxiously high volume, the only volume at which any teenager would listen. Rob walked over the poured snow-white cement slab that led to the edge of the pool. There, Dan and Sarah were splashing in the water, smacking each other in the head with long multicolored foam pool floats. Rob snuck a sidelong glance to admire Sarah in her shiny blue one-piece swimsuit, took three steps back and made a running leap into the pool. Landing in the midst of the two playing in the water, he surfaced and was instantly hit with a barrage from the foam toys. Taking a breath, he dove down, grabbed Dan by the ankles and pulled him under. Rob broke the water's surface just in time to hear Dan resurface, sputtering. He then turned his attention to Sarah. She could see the mischievous look in his eyes and began to swim toward the shallow end. "Oh, no you don't!" Rob cried as he dove toward her. Reaching out and grabbing her by one leg, he pulled her back. Playfully she fought back, splashing and kicking at until they were in the deepest part of the pool. She then changed her tactic and lunged at Rob, wrapping her arms and legs around his midsection, driving him under the water. Rob was taken aback by this move, pleasantly surprised by the forwardness of the maneuver but unnerved by being held underwater. He opened his eyes and saw her staring at him intently, and then her face began to move toward his.

The water around them was broken suddenly by another body that clamped a vice grip on Rob's shoulders. Terror gripped him as he forgot everything around him and suddenly began to fight toward the surface. Sarah released her grip the moment he began to frantically thrash. Dan however, would not be so easily shaken off, and held firm. In his frantic attempt to surface, Rob stomped his foot to the bottom of the pool to thrust himself to the surface. Unfortunately, he was standing directly over a plastic grate covering the suction for the pool filter. Pain shot up Rob's leg as the plastic grate broke from the force of his thrust, slicing open his foot.

The two shot to the surface like corks from a bottle. A small stream of blood followed like a ribbon stuck to Rob's foot. Wincing in pain, he made his way to the ladder and pulled himself out of the water. From her vantage point on the other side of the pool, Sarah could see that Rob was visibly shaken, and swam across to talk to him. It was not until she got closer that she saw the rivulets of blood streaming from his foot and began calling for help from Rob's mother who was in the house.

The world started to fade away into a gray mist, but Rob could still hear cries for help. "Rob! Rob! Are you okay? Please wake up. Help! Help!" The words cut their way through the fog in his brain, but his head was throbbing and he couldn't remember what happened. The flashing red and blue lights further increased the confusion when he attempted to crack open his eyes. Closing his eyes again, Rob tried to remember what was happening. The unrelenting cries continued and he wished that she would knock that shit off. Not only was it of no help whatsoever to his aching head, but it was distracting as hell. Tightly clamping his eyes closed while trying to ignore the world around him and his pounding headache, he concentrated on remembering how he got here.

After a few moments, and a few more agonized cries from the woman next him (Tiffany, that's her name!) the events of the last few hours came flooding back. Opening his eyes, Rob saw Tiffany look at him as she said, "Oh thank God! Hey! Please help! My friend is hurt and won't wake up!" The lights filled Rob's eyes yet again, and the realization that they were from a police car snapped into place. Were the cops here already? he asked himself. If they were then why the hell was Tiffany screaming to the people on the side of the road? Why wasn't the cop taking control of the situation? He looked closer, shielding his eyes from the light. The front end of the police cruiser was crumpled up against the front fender of the Volvo, which was in turn crushed into the guardrail of the bridge. He could see a large round crater in the windshield of the cop car, haloed in crimson blood. There was no movement inside the car. Great, he thought, a cop ran into us.

"Tiffany," he said quietly, "are you okay?"

She swung around in a flash, her eyes surveying Rob. "I'm fine, are *you* okay? I couldn't wake you up, I thought you were dead until I felt your pulse." She turned to look at the cop car. "That crazy cop ran right into us! He didn't even turn his lights on until after he hit us!" Rob was going to correct her, say that the cop probably hadn't turned them on but hit them in the accident, but he decided not to confuse the situation any further. Looking out where the driver's window had been, he could see about two feet of space between the door and the railing. He pushed the door and it only moved a few inches.

"Great," he said, "the damn door won't open."

"Just wait a minute, there are some people coming to help." She motioned dramatically out her window. Rob could see the figure of a large man coming toward them. It was difficult to see many details due to the flashing lights but the man looked to be wearing jeans and a button down shirt. Rob looked down and unbuckled his seat belt. A deflated and limp airbag hung into his lap from the steering wheel. Raising his hand to feel the back of his head, he winced as his hand passed over the sticky hair where his head had hit the window. Looking to his left and grabbing the door handle, he decided to try the door again. Using his shoulder and being careful not to hit his head, he managed to push the door open about a foot. Rob figured he could squeeze through, although it would be a tight fit. As he turned toward Tiffany and began to slide out the door, he saw that the man was only a few feet from the wrecked Volvo. In a brief flash of the lights, he could now see the man with more detail. He looked to be in his mid-twenties, and by his build could have easily been a linebacker for the Bucs. Rob saw the his shirt appeared to have a random pattern on it, probably one of those expensive designer shirts made to look old. A few seconds later when the lights flashed over the man again, Rob saw that unfortunately it was not some fancy pattern: it was blood. There was also a large fleshy gash behind a ragged hole in the man's jeans.

Tiffany was oblivious to the man's appearance and called enthusiastically to her rescuer, "Thank you! Please help us out of here, I think we are okay but we need to check on the Police Officer—." The man, who uttered a guttural growl, suddenly grabbed Tiffany's right arm, which had been resting on the sill of her window. He pulled with such strength and viciousness that she was lifted from her seat and slammed into the crumpled doorframe. She uttered a cry, more from confusion than pain, which then quickly transformed into a scream. The man hesitated for a moment and jerked again, causing Tiffany's face to contort in a mask of agony. Soft popping noises could be heard from her shoulder as it was pulled from the socket. She then heaved uncontrollably and emptied the remnants of beer and pepperoni pizza onto the door. Rob sat motionless, stunned at what was unfolding before him. The man then bent down and sunk his teeth into the top of Tiffany's forearm. The poor woman's howls of pain jolted Rob back into reality. Realizing he didn't have time to crawl out of the car and run to the passenger side and pull the man off, Rob looked for something to knock man away from Tiffany. The only thing within reach was the shotgun now propped against the center console. Grabbing the gun he thrust it through the window and aimed for the man's groin. The barrel hit dead center, but had no effect on the man. Rob tried again with the same result as the man bit deeper into the young woman's arm. He looked at Tiffany, who had stopped screaming, but was deathly pale and her eyes were beginning to roll back as she fought unconsciousness.

"Fucking let her go!" Rob screamed at the man to no avail. Blood was running down her dislocated arm from the man's gnawing and Rob pulled the shotgun against his shoulder. Pushing the safety off with his pointer finger, he quickly took aim at the man's chest and pulled the trigger. He was prepared for the muzzle flash and closed his eyes for a split second, but the report of the gun in the enclosed vehicle was deafening. The muffled silence that filled his ears after the report was a stark contrast to the surreal scene that followed. Rob saw a large crater surrounded by charred flash burns in the man's chest, and he was knocked back from the blast. The man held Tiffany's arm in his grasp for a moment, but was overcome from the force of the shot. She slid from his grip and his teeth left streaks in her flesh as he fell away. Her arm, jerked back by the motion, seemed to snap back into place as she fell back into her seat. Blood was streaming from the wound in her arm and Rob grabbed a sweatshirt from the backseat, pressing it against the wound. Placing her uninjured hand over the wound, he instructed her to hold it there to stop the bleeding.

Rob's mind was reeling. *What in the hell is going on?* he asked himself. Adrenaline filled his bloodstream and his nerves thrummed like a guitar string as he slammed his shoulder into the door. Paying no heed to his head wound, a lightning bolt of pain shot through his mind as he bumped his head on the frame of the car. Ducking through the window to reach back into the car, Rob grabbed his pack and shotgun, and made his way around to the passenger side. Setting the gun and pack on the roof of the damaged vehicle, he grasped the Volvo's door handle. It opened with surprising ease, and he momentarily lost his balance. Stumbling back, his foot hit the man on the ground and he instantly regained his balance. Walking the short distance back to the car, he could see Tiffany stirring. She was still holding the shirt onto the bite wound and was trying to gingerly move the arm. It seemed to hurt, but the fact that she could move it at all was a good sign. More than likely, the arm had popped back into joint when the man had fallen back. He leaned in to talk to her and was met with a muffled scream as she pointed with her good arm.

Rob whirled around to see the man, whose chest he had just cracked open, stand up and start stepping forward. "Jesus!" he screamed and grabbed the shotgun from the roof. Slamming the action back then forward, he ejected a shell casing and reloaded. He aimed yet again for center mass as he pulled the trigger. The round hit just to the left of the first wound, leaving another dark crimson hole in the man's chest. This time the man did not fall backwards but only stumbled, regaining his balance and starting back toward Rob. "Piss on it!" Rob screamed, chambered another round and took aim.

Rob was suddenly reminded of his childhood. His parents used to watch specials on cable from this comedian who used to hit watermelons with a sledgehammer. This is exactly what it looked like as the slug hit the man's skull. Rob caught a glimpse of a ghostly ridge of bone protrude from the back of the stump. Moments later, the body fell into a crumpled heap. His stomach lurched at the sight of the gore, and he turned to help Tiffany.

She was sitting with her legs out on the pavement and quietly sobbing. Bent over she was simultaneously attempting to cradle the wounded arm and keep pressure on the wound. Rob set the shotgun back onto the roof, picked up the pack and knelt down next to her. Opening the nylon bag, he searched and quickly found the multi-tool. "Let me see that," he said pointing to the sweatshirt. The shirt stuck to the wound and came off with a wet, crackling noise. The wound began to seep blood and the woman's already pale face went almost transparent from the sight. Working quickly, Rob opened the knife and cut the elastic bottom off of the sweatshirt. A second cut made the two-inch fabric strip into a crude bandage which he snuggly wrapped around the bite on her arm. Moving on, the remainder of the shirt was slit up the middle then down both sides of each sleeve. Cutting the sleeve off one of the halves, he tied it to the sleeve on the other half, forming a makeshift sling for Tiffany's injured arm. Looking up, he asked, "Do you think it's broken?"

"I don't think so. It's my shoulder that hurts." Tiffany winced as she moved her shoulder slightly.

"Good, I hoped it wasn't. I think your shoulder was just dislocated." Moving slowly so as to inflict as little pain as possible, Rob worked the sling under her injured arm. "This'll help support your arm so you don't have to keep holding it." Leaning in and pulling the other end up to her shoulder, he tied the two ends together. She slowly lowered her supporting arm to her lap, clenching her teeth until the injured arm was completely supported by the sling. Standing up, he questioned, "Can you walk?"

Leaning forward, Tiffany tried to stand, losing balance and bouncing off the doorframe. Before he could help, she steadied herself with the left arm, and stepped forward. "Yes, can we go back?"

Looking away, Rob stared out over the small channel that separated the island from the mainland. In the clear sky, the lights of the skyscrapers downtown could easily be seen. The waxing moon sent dim shadows dancing over the small waves in the watery void. Thoughts of the plan raced through his head. What did he expect to accomplish? Had he just really shot a man in the head? Turning around, he saw what had once been a beautiful young woman now a frightened child covered in her own blood. Enough was enough. It was time to stop putting other people's lives in danger. "Yes." Turning back, Rob reached out, his fingers meeting Tiffany's. "It is time to go home."

A sad smile spread across Tiffany's face. Leaning forward, she gently kissed Rob on the cheek. "Thank you… and I'm sorry."

A high-pitched growl echoed from the shadows of the hospital parking garage. Into the dim moonlight emerged a large old woman in a light purple mu-mu moving toward their position. To their right came a second deeper groan from a man in a Hawaiian shirt and khaki chinos. Both people seem to have the same blank expression as had the bloody mass at their feet. Tiffany let out a series of piercing cries. "Oh God! Oh God! Oh God!" Rob let her fingers slip from his. Slinging the pack over his right shoulder and picking up the shotgun in his left, he grasped Tiffany's hand again.

"We gotta keep moving. I'm sorry. We can't risk getting attacked by those… people." he said, gently tugging her toward the bridge. As if to emphasize the point, a third distinct growl echoed through the night to their rear. Moving together, they quickly shuffled their way over the gritty asphalt. The growls began fading as they increased the distance and followed the downward slope to Bayshore.

Rob and Tiffany stopped underneath the bridge for a moment to survey the area. On a normal night, this area would be bustling with activity from cars passing by with occasional catcall for the young lady at his side to couples walking under the lights of the long sidewalk that ran along the sea wall. There would perhaps be a Tampa socialite throwing a party for the privileged in their multi-million dollar bayside mansion. Even the occasional homeless guy would be seen panhandling for change.

Tonight however, there was uneasy silence. Abandoned cars were left at random intervals along the grassy shoulder and median, their drivers long gone. An overturned shopping cart lay near a cement park bench, spilling its accumulated treasures into the road. The darkness was palpable and only an occasional flickering light could be seen in the mansions along the boulevard. But what was most unnerving right now was the noise, specifically the lack thereof. With the hustle and bustle of daily life on this busy stretch of Tampa real estate, the sound of the bay was normally muted, even at this hour. With the normal routine having since been interrupted, the sound of the waves constantly crashing against the sea wall was an odd soundtrack to the evening.

Ensuring that there were no homicidal maniacs trying to viciously maim them ahead, they crossed the normally busy four-lane thoroughfare. Ascending the grassy hill on the other side to the cobblestone street at its top, the duo made their way to the next intersection. Pausing again to observe their surroundings, the words of Rob's mother to 'look both ways' made a sad smirk come to his face. His eyes started to water and lose focus. Bringing up his thumb and forefinger, he rubbed the moisture from the corners of his eyes. Turning to his left, the white Jeep could be seen just down the block. "Come on!" Rob said excitedly, pulling Tiffany on.

Rob fumbled with the keys in his pocket searching for the remote to unlock the doors as they approached the Jeep. The dull thump of the doors unlocking was a welcoming sound in the quiet night. Quickly making his way to the passenger side, he opened the door for Tiffany. The smell of oranges drifted out through the open door from the air freshener hanging below the rearview mirror. He gently guided Tiffany into the front seat, paying close attention not to accidentally nudge her wounded arm. Sliding past, the bandage covering the bite was soaked in dried blood. Red lines that looked like roads drawn on a map, streaked out from beneath the bandage. That's not good, he thought and closed the door. Jogging around to the other side, he jumped in the Jeep, locking the doors the minute the door slammed closed. Together they breathed a collective sigh of relief, relishing the relative safety of the SUV.

"How are you feeling?" Rob asked, staring out the front windshield.

"My shoulder still hurts like hell and my arm feels like it's on fire."

"Yeah, it looks like your arm is infected. I didn't think it could happen that quick." He sat quietly for a minute then asked, "So what the hell was wrong with those people?" Pausing, then howled, "I killed that guy… What… What.. I can't believe this… What the hell's going on?" he cried, losing his composure much to the dismay of the woman next to him.

"Rob, it's okay—."

"No it's not!" He sniffled hard, calming himself slightly. "But, I shot him three times. Twice in the chest…how the hell did he get back up?" His eyes grew wide and blood pounded in his head. Slamming his hands down onto the steering wheel causing a series of straining sounds from the steering column he screamed, "Twice in the chest with three inch mags... What the hell is going on?"

Tiffany scooted as far toward the side of the cab as her injured shoulder would allow. Tears began running down her cheeks. "Rob, please calm down. I need your help—."

Rob twisted his head angrily toward the pleading woman, eyes wide, like a cobra ready to strike. Before he unleashed a ferocious verbal attack, he looked at the scared woman, faltering. Get a hold of yourself man! The thought flashed into his mind, and the tension flowed out of his taut shoulders allowing his mind to focus. Tiffany began to quietly sob, and Rob reached over to touch her arm reassuringly. "I'm sorry. Shush. Hey, don't worry, we'll get through this."

"What do we do now?" she whimpered. "We can't go back home. We can't get out of the city; they said so on the radio. So what do we do now?" The last word seemed to echo in the enclosed space of the SUV and they both looked out the Jeep's windshield onto the silent street. It could have been just any weekday night in the quiet neighborhood. A slight breeze off the water blew leaves across the cobblestone street. The oak's branches swayed gently, oblivious and waving to the stars.

Rob pulled out his cell phone and tossed it onto the dimpled grey plastic of the dashboard. Picking up the keys from the center console, he slid one into the ignition and twisted the switch to accessory. Glowing to life, the radio displayed it was still tuned to the local AM talk station before switching to the time. Twelve o'clock. Huh, the last time he remembered looking at a clock was almost two hours ago when he had last spoken to Sarah. Christ, those *things* must be what is attacking everyone on MacDill. "Here's what we're going to..." Rob was cut short by the raspy radio announcer.

"...have confirmed reports that the violence has spread from the local hospitals to the surrounding communities. We have been trying to contact anyone at either University or General Hospitals. There has been no further comment from FEMA, DHS or Tampa Emergency Management as to what is being done to control this violence. All we can do is suggest that if you are near an area hospital try to get inside and stay in your homes. If you do try to evacuate, be careful. We have had unconfirmed reports that there have been shootings at quarantine checkpoints and people trying to run through with their vehicles.

I will be here all night, giving you the latest information as it comes in, taking calls and emails from listeners. I have an email here from Steve in south Tampa, near MacDill. It says, 'Mac, I hope you read this on the air and it helps keep everyone safe. I do not consider myself a violent man but I do what I have to do to protect my family. I live near Ballast point and earlier tonight I heard explosions and gunshots from the south. My wife was trying to distract the children and keep them from getting upset, but the noise kept getting louder. I took out my .45 just in case. Janie put my children to bed a short time later and we continued to follow the news in the living room. Suddenly, I heard a banging in the back yard and I looked out the window to see a woman struggling to get over our small fence. I walked to the back door figuring the gun would scare her off. When I opened the back door, the woman who was now standing in my backyard, growled like a dog. The next thing I knew, she sprinted across the lawn and tried attacking me. Grabbing at me, scratching at my body and at one point even biting! I was able to push her back into the yard, waving my gun and yelling for her to leave. She came at me again and I shot her in the leg. She stumbled for a moment, growled even louder, and kept coming. I then shot her in the chest causing her to fall backwards into the yard. At this point I tried to go in and call the police. I heard grunting from behind me and swung around just as I was attacked again! She bit me on the arm, and scratched the hell out of my face. I pushed her away and fired. I don't know how many shots I fired. I think five but in my frenzy only one of them hit her. I will never forget the sight of what that bullet did to that crazed woman's head. But at least she didn't get up.

So to make a long story short: if you have to attack one of these people, shoot them in the head.'

Ummm, thanks Steve, but I don't think I can advocate shooting anyone. Perhaps that will help our law enforcement officers out there…"

The cell phone on the dash suddenly lit up the windshield, vibrating vigorously across the dash. Rob eyed it warily, picking it up and examining the screen. A small blue WiFi icon shone brightly in the corner of the screen. A chat request from Sarah flashed on the small LCD. Accepting the request, words immediately flashed up on the screen.

"WHERE RU?!"

"On way, was attacked" he typed.

"RU OK?

"Yes, fine. I now know what you were talking about."

"YES, BE CAREFUL! PLZ HURRY!"

Looking over as he slid the cell phone into his pocket, he could see Tiffany staring transfixed at the green LEDs on the radio face. Rob reached out and gently touched her shoulder. She flinched away and then relaxed, turning to look at him sheepishly. "Hey," he said gently, "here's what we are going to do. We need to get you some help. It's not safe at any hospital, but I think you will be alright for the time being." He lied. "I think it would help to have Sarah. Maybe we can even find a medic on the base."

In the fog of her mind, she managed, "But what about those, er, people? I mean she's trapped, right?"

"Yes and that is why we are going to help her. That way you can get some help and she can get out of there."

Tiffany moaned and again slouched toward the door.

"You won't even have to leave the car, I have a plan."

She twisted to look at him, mind momentarily clearing and spat, "A plan! Oh really? Just like the plan that we had just to drive to your car?" She lifted her arm with her left, "And look where that got us."

"That wasn't my fault! I didn't—"

"SHUT UP!" she yelled and began raggedly breathing. "I don't care why it happened, but it happened. Now we are heading off to save some bitch when we should be trying to get the fuck outta dodge!" Gasping now for breath, she grabbed Rob's arm. "I am going with you to get her because now I have no choice. But if we can't help her, we leave! OK?" She leaned heavily on him, chest heaving and lips beginning to go pale in the dim light.

"Calm down! Come on now, breath slowly, in and out." Steadying his breath, Rob coached her to follow suit. The heaving in her chest slowed, and soon their breathing had matched a steady, even pace. "Now, like I said, we are going to pick up Sarah and she is going to help. I want you just to try to relax." Flipping on the dome light, Rob reached over to help her with the seat belt. Reaching around the sling to get to the nylon belt, the flesh on Tiffany's arm caught his attention. What had once been a golden tan forearm with smooth, creamy skin had become gray and almost transparent. Veins and arteries could be seen crisscrossing underneath the pale skin and had a yellow tinge tapering to a gray where it met the bloody bandage. The red streaks that had only a few minutes ago been roughly six inches in length now ran all the way up her bicep, disappearing under the cuff of her t-shirt. Trying not to stare or jostle the arm, he gently pulled the belt across and secured it with a click. Who the hell am I kidding, he thought, Sarah's frantic pleas almost assured there would be no medical personnel to help, but what was the alternative? An overused old adage came to mind. 'In times of trouble go with what you know.' Focusing on those words steadied his resolve

Sitting back, Rob told Tiffany, "Hold on. We may have to go over a curb or two," and started the engine. Turning on the headlights bathed the cab in the glow from the instrument cluster, momentarily blinding the two passengers. As their eyes adjusted, the figure of a middle-aged woman was illuminated by the headlights. The woman was wearing a navy blue skirt and white shirt that was covered in blood. She was standing lopsidedly on one high heel and one bare foot, and snarled in the glow of the headlights. The source of the blood looked to be a bullet hole to the chest, exactly where her heart *should* have been. While the blood covering her chest was a dull purplish red and coagulated, her body glistened candy apple red. Rob put the Jeep into gear and stomped the accelerator just as the woman rapidly closed the distance between them in an awkward hobble-run. The Jeep swerved to the right attempting to move out of the path of the advancing woman. A parked car on the opposite side of the street prevented the vehicle from avoiding the advancing woman, and Rob cringed as he heard a wet thump from the front fender. Oh great, double homicide, he thought to himself darkly. But somehow deep down inside he had the sickening idea that these people were already dead. The Jeep's wheels spun on the slick cobblestone road as Rob turned the car toward the bay.

Coming to the intersection of Bayshore, the vehicle slowed while turning south along the boulevard. Here and there abandoned vehicles blocked individual lanes causing Rob to make wide arcs as he drove. The dim orange glow of the streetlights illuminating the seaside-walking path cast long shadows across the dark pavement. Up ahead, a black Porsche SUV with its passenger door open blocked their forward progress. Traveling at a slightly faster than a jogging pace, Rob swerved around the vehicle and continued further down the dark road. Moments later at a three-way intersection, a large water truck had careened into a signal pole (why the truck was on the road was a riddle in itself: trucks weren't allowed on the scenic drive) and been hit by several cars creating a makeshift roadblock. The Jeep slowed and turned over the curb onto the grassy median. Tiffany moaned briefly as her head bounced forward then back with the rocking motion of the vehicle. Catching the exaggerated motion out of the corner of his eye, Rob looked over to just catch sight of the whites of her eyes rolling back into her head. Her left arm then fell away from where it had been supporting the injured right, and she slumped against the doorframe. The truck skid to a stop in the grass as Rob leaned over.

"Tiffany, Tiffany?" he asked softly as he lifted her good arm off the seat and gently held her hand. "Can you hear me?" She did not stir. After waiting a few moments, he swallowed hard and shifted the limp hand to feel for a pulse. The absence of the steady rhythmic beat confirmed his fears. "No!" he shouted, "NO! NO!" The cab of the Jeep filled with his cries and the loud thump-thump-thump as he repeatedly slammed his fists on to the steering wheel. Inadvertently, the horn bleated out an irregular tune as Rob's right palm glanced the button. Grasping the steering wheel in his hands, knuckles turning bright white under the strain, he tried to slow the wheezing by puffing through his clenched teeth. In the rearview mirror, chalky, glazed eyes gleamed in the dim green light of the dash. There was nothing more he could do for her. He clenched his eyes closed to fight the tidal wave of emotions that suddenly rushed over him. Why did I let her come along? All she wanted was my protection! Opening his eyes, he looked out onto the large sculpture to the right. His breathing slowed again and thoughts began to coherently coalesce once more. It was not my fault; I tried to stop her. She insisted on coming with. He hesitated. But did I try hard enough? Roughly shaking his head in an attempt to physically push the thoughts out of his mind, Rob absently depressed the accelerator. Tiffany's body bounced against the side of the Jeep when they descended the curb and settled back as the vehicle found the northbound lane.

CHAPTER EIGHT

The snail's pace required to avoid various obstructions seemed to take an eternity. The cars and trucks that were strewn about the lanes made Rob think of all those post apocalyptical movies he had seen over the years. What's next, he thought, locusts and brimstone?

Traveling south, the normally regal houses that lined the boulevard started to lose their stately looks. Many windows on the first floors had been broken out, several doors had been left open, and he even saw two groups of people run out of one house with apparently no regard as to what they were leaving behind. He was paying such close attention to this last event that he did not notice the dark blue Honda civic sitting directly in the Jeep's path. In his peripheral, he caught sight of the car just seconds before a collision. Even though the truck had been moving slowly, the accident could have damaged the radiator or some other vital component. Having the Jeep become incapacitated was unthinkable. Rob swerved to the right, inertia causing their bodies to slump to the left. The Jeep's wheels then struck the curb on the turning lane, forcing the Rob and the body to swing back towards the right as he fought to right the vehicle's path.

From across the front seat, Rob did not notice the loud purr that drifted through the truck's interior, as he was preoccupied with fighting the wheel and looking out to avoid any further obstacles. Tiffany's left arm jerked spasmodically and settled back onto the seat. The fingers then methodically closed and reopened as the arm jerked awkwardly toward the dead woman's lap. The Jeep stopped swerving and settled into the far left lane, slowing to a crawl. Rob inhaled deeply, releasing the tension in his body with a whistle as he exhaled. A thick film of sweat covered his upper body, and he reached over to turn up the air conditioning.

A hand shot across the Jeep and tightly grasped his forearm. "What the hell?" Rob asked in surprise. He turned and looked directly into Tiffany's expressionless face. The soft features suddenly twisted into a mask of rage as she growled and lunged across the cab, as her bad arm grabbed for his chest. Caught by surprise,

Rob stomped his foot on the accelerator. Pressing against the door, he twisted his body while holding on which caused the steering wheel to jerk left. The sudden momentum and change in direction flung Tiffany back across the Jeep. The crack of skull meeting with the passenger window made Rob wince even as he fought to control the vehicle. Through the windshield, the ornate white cement retaining wall quickly filled the view. Rob yanked the wheel to the right and slammed on the brakes. The truck changed direction slightly, and was now in a power slide heading toward a gap in the wall. "FUCK!" he screamed as the front of the SUV slammed into the far pillar at an angle, causing the airbag to deploy. Rob's already injured head was forced into the headrest, as bright spots exploded in his vision as the earlier head wound made contact. The rear of the Jeep then slid into the opposite pillar, the sustained force pushing the front of the Jeep through the gap. The front wheel slid off into the void, the friction of metal cement finally stopping the vehicle with an ear-splitting screech.

The world swam before Rob's eyes, threatening to disappear completely. Letting out a muffled groan, he tried to push both the white fabric and acrid odor of the airbag out of his face. To the right, a flurry of frantic activity erupted as Tiffany, or whatever was left of her, fought the restraints. It seemed to completely forget Rob, who even in his grogginess had still had the presence of mind to unlatch his seatbelt. It seemed to notice the movement and began to wildly strike out in his direction, grabbing and growling with no apparent thought. Pressing himself against the door, he quickly pulled the door handle. Balance almost failed him as he leaned out precariously, catching himself in time to prevent a face plant onto the steps below. Spinning head notwithstanding, Rob slid out onto the stairs. One arm and leg touched the solid ground before he slithered the rest of the way to the waiting cement. The stench of rotting fish and plant life hit almost immediately and he was overcome with nausea, dry heaving several times before controlling the urge. The Tiffany-thing seemed to sense that he had left the Jeep and began thrashing even more wildly, whining loudly into the empty cab. Taking a shallow breath, Rob turned and opened the back door to grab the pack from the back seat. There on the floor behind the passenger sat the bag containing his supplies and more importantly, all his ammunition. He cursed himself quietly; he left the shotgun on the floor in front of Tiffany. No helping it now, he thought, and I sure as hell am not going in after it. Standing as tall as he could, Rob reached across the backseat to grab the bag. Tips of fingers slid under the nylon loop at the top of the bag, and as it was dragged across the backseat, a pale hand struck the bag. Instantly grasping the black bag, a groan of eerie triumph called out over the calm water. "No way!" Rob yelled, taking a stronger hold of the bag and throwing his body away from the wounded vehicle. There was an unzipping sound as the things fingers lost grip and suddenly broke loose. Rob, unable this time to compensate for the sudden change in direction, fell backward down the stairs into the water below.

The water was only a couple feet deep, but was filled with large rocks strategically placed as a surf break. The rocks bit into Rob's hands and buttocks as he desperately attempted to break his fall. Trying to yelp in pain, water filled his mouth and he was only able to utter a garbled groan. Sputtering, his feet finally found purchase and Rob stood unsteadily on the slick rocks. An angry growl from the direction of the sea wall echoed out over the still bay waters. Outlines of several figures could be seen silhouetting against the orange light of the street lamps. Bobbling around like cartoons, they walked back and forth next to the cement rail, appearing to search out a way out onto the water. A pair of figures collided, sending the one nearest Rob cart wheeling into the water with a splash. Startled, Rob jumped back and almost lost his footing once again. As the thing tried to stand, a large bloodstain could be seen running down the small white t-shirt, continuing down the leg of a short plaid skirt and ending on the legs of what had been an attractive young woman. The thing slipped, fell and tried to regain its footing. A fresh cut appeared on its forehead from striking the rocks. Again and again it thrashed and growled as it tried desperately to make its way toward Rob. This, in turn, caused the things on the sidewalk above to become more and more agitated, growling loudly into the night, movements becoming more fiercely chaotic.

Rob, sensing the moment was right, grabbed the black nylon bag and began wading his way south toward the direction of the base. Moving slow and deliberate as to not make much noise or cause too large a disturbance in the water, he chanced a look over his shoulder just as another body fell into the water. The body of a short obese man fell onto the young woman and the two submerged, quickly resurfacing in a jumble of arms and legs. Quietly, Rob gave thanks for their inability to maneuver the rocky bottom of the bay and continued toward the base.

The walk was slow going. Every fifty feet or so a rock would grab hold of his pant leg causing him to flinch as the exposed skin would be scrapped away and the wound burning from the salt water. Just a little further, Rob kept saying to himself, focusing on this mantra to ignore the pain. While this helped dull the pain somewhat, the loss of concentration on the task at hand caused him to slip on the slick algae covered rock. Rolling his ankle, he winced and he caught his footing just before the ankle was twisted far enough to strain. Breathing a sigh of relief, Rob then shifted his focus back to walking, one foot in front of the other toward the goal. The sloshing of his legs carefully moving through the water, faint screams, groans and erratic gunfire filled the night. The gunshots seemed to trigger a nagging idea in his mind that he could not quite place. Taking several more quiet steps, the connection clicked together in his mind. "Oh shit." Rob murmured out loud. His right hand shot to the holster on his hip, fingers sliding over the nylon straps to the handle of the Barretta, which was tacky from the drying seawater. "Sonovabitch."

Most modern handguns are designed to withstand extended exposure to moisture, such as firing in the rain or even the occasional dunking that may occur in the course of their use. Additionally, modern ammunition is sealed tight enough that unless submerged for an extended period of time, their effectiveness should not be affected by exposure. The major difference becomes whether the weapon is exposed to salt water or fresh water. A well-kept weapon that is regularly cleaned and oiled should be able to fare well with just about any exposure to fresh water. Salt water however is a different story. Unless timely cleaning occurs shortly after submergence, the weapon can become useless.

This ran through Rob's mind as he pulled his backpack off his shoulder, opening the bag to pull a bottle of water out of his pack. Putting the bottle under his arm, he pulled out the Barretta, ejecting the magazine into his palm. Rob then grabbed the bottle of water, twisted off the cap, and poured the water over the weapon and clip until empty. Dropping the bottle into the water, he diligently shook the weapon and clip to remove any remaining water. The clip was then slid back into the Barretta. That is the best I can do right now, he thought to himself. As the weapon was replaced in the holster, Rob's hand brushed a lump in his pocket and he suddenly remembered his cell phone. Pulling the wet phone out of his pocket, he pushed the center directional button on the keypad to illuminate the screen. When nothing happened, Rob tried the power button hoping that the phone had just turned off. Again, nothing happened. "Fuck!" he cursed, phone dropping from his fingers and into the bay below. This was going to made finding Sarah a whole lot more difficult.

There were less and less rocks on the floor of the bay as the end of the seawall and accompanying sidewalk could be seen up ahead. Marked by a small condo that was built on the shoreline just beyond the wall, he approached the end and the stench of rotting seaweed became almost unbearable. Rob began to sink into the thick muck as he reached the shoreline and dragged himself up onto the solid ground. There was a single light on in the condo that faintly illuminated the grassy knoll behind the building. Rob carefully surveyed the area, watching closely for any movement and listening intently for the telltale growl of the things. While the noise continued to be heard in the distance, nothing moved and Rob lowered his guard slightly. Looking down, his boots were covered in a thick layer of mud, which he began wiping off on the grass, legs stinging as the jeans shifted under his movements. A window slid open with a thud and Rob looked up to see a middle aged man pointing a large rifle in his direction. "Get the hell out of here," bellowed the voice of the man in the window.

Rob put his hands up and said, "I don't want any trouble. I—."

The man cut him off. "I don't give a shit if you are selling fucking Mary Kay, get the hell out of my yard!"

"Okay, Okay, I am going!" Rob replied and quickly jogged to the edge of the yard. The barrel of the rifle tracked him closely until he reached the edge of the building. After making his way to the front and scanning the area, no obvious signs of danger were apparent. With this, he sprinted to take cover under a large southern oak tree in the next yard over. Glancing over his shoulder, the man in the front window lowered the rifle, closed the window and snuffed the light.

The boulevard was flanked on either side by large trees and lit by the occasional old-fashioned streetlight. The houses on both sides of the street were dark with the exception of the one building he had just passed. With only a few short miles to the base, Rob looked around to find a means of transport. Several cars lined the street, one or two with the doors ajar and the dome light's glowing dimly as their batteries ran down. Approaching several of these, the keys could not be found in the ignition and were not anywhere in the vicinity. On the sidewalk next to a crimson stain, a pink bicycle with plastic tassels hanging lifelessly from the handlebars was a grim reminder that even children were not immune to the day's events. The sight of the bike gave Rob an idea. Thepeople in this part of town loved to ride their bicycles on the eight-mile sidewalk on sunny Florida afternoons, therefore there should be a bicycle or two to be found. After a few minutes of furtive searching, and the increased growling of the things in the distance, he resolved himself that his own two feet were to be his transport.

Could anything actually go right today? he thought to himself as he tightened the straps of the pack onto his shoulders and fastened the waist strap securely around his midsection. With a slight hop as a start, Rob began to jog down the road toward MacDill.

Although he was already damp from his escapades in the bay, the combination of the moist heavy clothing and stiflingly humid night air caused rivulets of sweat to run down Rob's body. In the background, sounds of gunshots, growls and breaking glass increased their frequency as he closed on the Base. Buildings on either side of the lane were all dark now, and many had all the windows on the lower levels broken in, their curtains hanging limply out of the windows. The road ahead was lit by a flickering yellow glow. Drawing nearer, Rob could see that it was a large colonial mansion, one of the many that lined the bay, had caught on fire. A solitary Tampa Fire Department pumper truck was parked in front of the house. Hoses were run from a nearby fire hydrant to the truck, and various firefighting gear could be seen strewn about the front yard in the light of the blaze. Slowing, he was unable to locate any firefighters. As Rob leapt over the canvas hose that ran across the road, a growl could be heard from the direction of the fire truck and he caught a glimpse of movement from the corner of his eye. His body was beaten and tired, but at that moment adrenaline again filled his veins. Lowering his head, he put on a burst of speed and ran, widening the distance from the flaming wreckage.

***

"Attention everyone, we will be landing in a few moments. Mr. Leske, if you could come to the cockpit for a moment?" The pilot's voice, slow and monotone, sounded over the Gulfstream's PA.

Chad looked up from his laptop, irritated that he was interrupted so close to finishing the initial portion of his operational report. Huffing and unbuckling his seatbelt, he slid out from behind the plush leather seat. Casting a glance to ensure the briefcase was still on the next seat, he walked toward the faux wood paneled door that lead to the cockpit.

Rapping on the door, a muffled 'enter' replied from the other side. Opening the door, Chad was slightly taken aback by the myriad of display screens and gauges. Then asked with annoyance, "Captain, what can I help you with?"

"Sir," the captain replied unperturbed. He had dealt with many of these bureaucrats and had developed a thick skin for their idiosyncrasies. "We cannot get a response from MacDill tower, with Tampa approach knocked out and the no fly order, the closest airport is PIE across the water."

Chad, not to be kept from his job by some whiney pilot, looked out the windscreen. The Air Force base was lit up like Christmas. Even from this distance, he could see the lights of the runway. "Well, it doesn't look like anything is out of the ordinary. Why don't you try calling again?"

The captain hit the transmit button and spoke into his mic, "MacDill Tower, this is Heath One Niner, do you copy, over?" He listened for a minute while Chad tapped his thumb rhythmically on the copilot's seat. "Sir, I am still getting no response from MacDill. We need to divert—."

Chad cut him off curtly. "Captain, you will do no such thing! This is a national emergency." He thought for a moment, and then came up with one of his always-ingenious ideas. "Why don't you fly over the base and see if there is something wrong with the runway. If not, you can come back and land!" Chad smiled, pleased with himself.

"Sir, that is not a good idea and very dangerous. We don't know what is going on down there. There could be an accident or some other—."

"Listen, Captain," Chad interrupted again, "I am acting on behalf of the Director of the CDC, who is following the direct orders of the President." Continuing in a smug tone, "Therefore, I order you to do whatever you have to do to determine there is no immediate danger and then land this aircraft. Do you understand?"

The pilot sat in silence for a moment, absently checking and rechecking the various readings in the cockpit. Sighing, he said, "Yes sir, I understand. But I am going on record right now that this is a very bad decision and against FAA regulations."

"Duly noted Captain, I will add that to my report. How long until we can expect to be on the ground?"

"Well, it will take us several minutes to do the fly over then line up again for approach. I would estimate twenty minutes."

"Very good!" Chad said in a suddenly chipper tone. "I will see you on the ground then." He turned, exiting the cockpit and closing the door behind. The blue sport coat was still slung over the back of his seat when he slid down and belted in. Now I can finish this report before landing, he thought to himself. The Director is going to want it sent the minute the wheels are down.

Happily typing away, the pilot's announcement about landing, were summarily ignored as the pitch change of the plane's droning engines and the clunk of landing gear maneuvered into position. Chad's stomach fluttered slightly while the Gulfstream lost altitude on their final approach and he closed the lid of the laptop in preparation. When the jarring bumps of the wheels touching the tarmac and the roar of the engines reversing signaled touchdown, he unbuckled the safety belt.

Suddenly, as the plane slowed, a loud explosion followed by the sounds of flying metal filled the cabin. Loud alarm sirens could be heard through the cockpit doors as the pilots fought to keep the aircraft straight down the runway. Out the window, the port engine was engulfed in smoke as the fire suppression system attempted to prevent the further ignition of jet fuel.

Chad's eyes widened as his stomach suddenly seemed to drop through the floor. Clenching the table in an attempt to steel himself, he tried to use his normally calculating mind to put the situation neatly in a box. The wheels rolled to a stop and he stood up immediately. "Open up that door," he called to one of the technicians, "we need to get everyone off this plane!" Yes, he thought to himself, this was the right thing to do. Smiling in self-satisfaction, metal briefcase in one hand and laptop in the other, he made his way to the door and onto the runway.

After moving a few yards from the injured aircraft and looking back, the engine could be seen scorched and filling their noses with acrid smoke. Below, a strange pile of debris sat smoldering. Chad took several steps forward to further investigate the strange debris, curiosity getting the better of him. "Christ," he said to himself as he looked at the pile, "is that an arm?"

Calls of several of the medical personnel to the ground crew interrupted his investigation and he turned to see several flight suit clad individuals running towards the group. See, all's well that ends well, he thought in satisfaction. Watching the ground crew as they approached, something suddenly did not seem right. Maybe it was their gait, he thought until the first individual approached the group. Dark stains could be seen covering the front of the flight suit and the young man launched himself at the nearest member of his team. The unsuspecting woman screamed in surprise as she was knocked to the ground, then gurgled as her nose was ripped out in the man's teeth. Several others of the team stood like statues, watching as their colleague was torn apart by the monster and did not see their own deaths approaching. Chad watched the scene in terror, a hot stream of urine running down the inside of his thighs.

Losing control of all but the most primal instincts, he threw down the laptop and sprinted away. Tucking the briefcase under his arm like a football (he would never lose something as important as this, he thought, barely coherent) Chad looked for somewhere to hide. The animalistic growls, screams of pain and gunshots followed him into the dark night.

CHAPTER NINE

A gate that guarded the entrance to the base could be seen in the distance illuminated by the dim light of the house fire. Instead of being a secure checkpoint preventing unauthorized entry to the installation, it had the appearance of a scrap yard left to waste. Getting closer, Rob could see that the cement barricades preventing traffic from either entering or leaving the base were raised. On those same barricades, several vehicles were crumpled from the driver's attempts to run the gates. A small white hatchback lay on its back blocking the oncoming lane, almost comically resembling a dead beetle.

Rob slowed to a walk, catching his breath before approaching the crumpled wrecks. After the events of the evening, he decided on being very cautious with this new situation. Broken safety glass littered the lane, reflecting the faint firelight and crunching softly under the approaching footsteps. There was a small gap between a crumpled red H2 and yellow

Suburban on its side. Rob sucked in his stomach, squeezed through and then leaped over the cement barricade to enter the base. To the right, another small aluminum and bulletproof glass security booth lay in a broken pile to the right of the gate. The front tires of a large U-Rent-It truck rested on the wreckage. One of the base security vehicles, a Blazer painted in desert cammo and security forces crest on the side, stood parked neatly in the designated parking spot. From the skid marks on the pavement, the truck missed being hit by less than a foot. Rob stepped closer to the destroyed booth and eyed a leg sticking out from beneath a sheet of aluminum. Stepping cautiously toward the limb he quietly called, "Hey, you okay?" No response. Several tense seconds later, he reached out to nudge the leg and call again. There were again no stirrings from the leg or body beneath the sheet. Sighing in relief, he bent down, grabbing the sheet of metal to shift it off the body and into the ditch. Rob took a discretionary step back to analyze what he saw.

All that was left of the left side of the man's face was gore, probably the result of being struck by the truck resting on the remains of the guard shack. The other eye stared lifelessly into the dark Florida night. Rob grimaced at the sight. Several heartbeats later, he reached out a tentative hand to left side of the man's throat, avoiding the gore just above his wrist. The cool, clammy flesh gave under the fingers as he searched for the beating of the man's heart to no avail. Reaching over, Rob closed the man's open eye and glanced at the uniform again as he stood. The nametape on the man's left chest read 'Alverez' and by the stripes on his arm, he was a Tech Sergeant. Rob noticed that Alverez looked to be about his size. The realization that wet jeans clung to his legs and soggy boots encased his feet like wet concrete gave him a morbid idea. He looked around and listened intently. While the sounds of gunshots and growls could be heard nearby, they didn't seem to be coming toward his location. Working quickly, Rob removed the dead airman's boots and socks. He then stripped off the man's ABU bottoms and duty belt that held Alverez' M9 and extra ammunition. Kicking off his shoes, he pulled off the wet pants and skivvies, tossing them into the nearby ditch and swiftly dressed in the new clothes. Fastening the belt around his waist, Rob took the M9 pistol out of its holster, checked the clip and chamber to ensure that it was loaded. Replacing it, he bent down to pick up the pack when something caught his eye. About ten feet further into the ditch, a short antenna-like item was sticking straight into the air. Walking over, Rob saw an M4 assault rifle wedged into the dirt of the ditch. Smiling, he picked up the weapon. Following the same ritual, Rob checked to ensure the weapon was loaded, and then chambered a round.

In the near distance, the clack-clack-clack of rifle fire and frantic yelling could be heard. Rob held the rifle at his side, turning to move toward the sound when the gun bounced off his thigh with a metallic chink. He shifted the rifle and shoved his unburdened hand into his pocket. Clammy fingers met with the familiar ridges of keys and pulled them out into sight. The faint outline of "GM" could be seen on the keys, and Rob gave a silent cheer. It's about goddamn time something went my way, he thought and ran over to the security forces Blazer. Getting in, Rob jammed the key into ignition and was rewarded by the roar of the engine as it sprang to life. Switching on the lights as he placed the truck in reverse, he then checked the rearview mirror. Rob had just enough time to see another uniformed person, this time a young woman with an arm missing from her uniform, before the vehicle impacted with a slimy thump.

"Shit!" Rob yelled as the woman's head smacked against the rear window, leaving a dark smudge from the impact. He threw the vehicle into drive and pulled around to take a look, hoping to God that it was one of those things. The alternative sent a cold shiver down his spine. Through the driver's side window the woman was thrashing to get up. Her remaining arm was bent at an unnatural angle and skin was scraped off the side of her face to expose the muscle beneath. The woman's mouth contorted into an animalistic growl. "Well, thank God for small favors," he said aloud, turning to look forward.

The lights of the truck illuminated the carnage he pulled slowly away from the gate. Bodies were strewn across the landscape; from the road ahead to the lawns of the buildings as he passed. Blood pooling around the bodies seemed to absorb the light of the headlamps in an inky blackness. Several fires could be seen burning, partially obscured by the buildings, at various points on the base. As Rob made his way through the wasteland, a loud thump to his right jerked him from his reverie. A young man just past adolescence, wearing a white uniform pocked with several small caliber bullet holes, was beating on the passenger side window. Rob instinctively hit the automatic door lock and was about to speed up when he heard a loud crack from the front of the Blazer. He only had time enough to see a skull bounce off where it had hit the hood as the rest of the body was pulled under the moving vehicle. Accelerating, several figures had heard the disturbance and were now moving quickly toward the vehicle. The Blazer swerved to avoid hitting as many as possible, but it seemed that for every four 'things' avoided, one would bounce off the side or front fenders. It was difficult to hear their growls until the truck was almost on top off them and every time Rob heard them, it made his skin crawl.

Up ahead, flashes of light lit the night and the staccato of rifle fire thrummed inside the vehicle. Rob could see a figure in the intermittent light firing at the things and bodies dropping with every muzzle flash. Closing the distance, the bodies were swarming toward the figure as one spent magazine was replaced by another, depleting the defender's supply.

Rob could make out that the figure was a male wearing a black 'SF' armband in desert cammo's, standing next to a steel utility shack and efficiently dropping any threat within 30 yards. The airman, seeing the Blazer, hesitated a moment to wave frantically and then returned to firing at the threat. Rob turned the wheel to the right, bringing the wheels of the SUV up and over the curb with a jarring series of bumps. This sent the microphone to the security radio soaring though the air, clipping him beneath the jaw and causing him to snap his jaws together on his tongue. Cursing softly, he aimed the nose of the vehicle directly toward the airman, centering him in the headlights of the truck. Dozens of bodies were either caught in the path or stepped in front of the moving vehicle, slamming into the front end of the SUV. Blood hemorrhaged into random patterns onto the plastic grill and bumper, shattering the front of the vehicle as it mowed down the bodies approaching the airman's position. Closing within several car lengths of the lone man, Rob stepped on the brake and twisted the wheel to send the vehicle into a power skid. The SUV's rear end skidded to a stop against the utility shed with a loud clang, triggering an almost simultaneous growl from all the bodies around their position. The airman broke into a sprint as soon as the Blazer came to a rest. Rob slapped the unlock button to open the doors as the man reached the door handle. Jumping in, the airman slammed the door closed behind him and yelled, "DRIVE!"

Needing no encouragement, Rob jammed the accelerator down and created another path of destruction through the bodies. By the time the four wheels had again made contact with asphalt by pulling back on to the main road, a red film completely covered the windshield giving everything a pink hue. Rob switched the windshield washers on in a vain attempt to clear the sticky gore off the window and only managed to smear large tracks into the blood. Turning to the man, he asked, "You okay?" as he squirted more washer fluid onto the streaked glass.

"Yes sir. But damn that was close." the man replied in a thick Tennessee accent, "I thought I was done fer." He looked Rob over quick, noting the ABU pants and black surf T-shirt, then asked, "Where the hell did you come from?"

Rob snorted, "Yeah, well, it's a long story." Driving under a streetlamp, he noticed the nametag and the stripes on the man's uniform and said, "Listen Tech Sergeant Dillingham, I'll have to explain later. But right now I need to know two things: Do you have any idea what is going on and what can you tell me about the utility buildings around the airfield?"

The sergeant's eyes narrowed as he said, "Mister, I have no damn clue as to what is going on. But why do you want to know about the airfield? By the look of you, you ain't even supposed to be—."

"You're right, I am not supposed to be here!" Rob slowed the vehicle to a stop under the next streetlamp. "Look, my friend is in the guard and was on duty tonight. She called me a couple of hours ago begging frantically for help. She said the base was being attacked by the wounded that were brought in and that she is hiding in a building near the airfield." He looked at the sergeant. "I don't know how your night has been going but I can tell you mine has been absolute dog shit. So, I need your help. I'm not some terrorist; in fact I just got out of the Navy. So, at least point me in the right direction. I think you owe me that much."

A loud smack filled the cab as a fist hit the rear window of the Blazer. "Drive son!" Dillingham demanded. The vehicle jumped forward and the things' growls faded beneath the hum of the engine. "Alright, I guess we can sort this all out later. But don't you get your hopes too high. I don't think there is anybody left to find to tell you the truth. I haven't heard anything on the radio for an hour or so. Hell, if I didn't have to piss so bad I would still be hugging a pipe in that metal shack. Hot as hell in there, let me tell you." He leaned over and turned up the air conditioning. "Turn here," he said as he pointed. "So, you know my name. What's yours?"

"Rob Cohen."

"Okay Rob, here's what I know. Shit hit the fan this afternoon since that bomb destroyed the airport. They put us on ThreatCon and FPCON Delta immediately, then SOCOM and SPECOM locked down tighter than a virgin on prom night. They started bringing casualties to the base hospital shortly after that. On roving watch a while later, we heard calls for security back up at the hospital. I figured some of the walking wounded they had brought in had decided to get fussy and the doctors over at the hospital didn't feel like dealing with them. We sent another unit to the hospital after the first team called for backup. About a half hour or so after that, we were sending units all over the base but no word from the units at the hospital." Dillingham shifted uncomfortably in his seat. "I went out to put some eyes on the situation, not those damn closed circuit cameras. Not fifteen minutes out on my patrol all hell broke loose. Folks were runnin' out of the buildings screaming and I could hear gunshots. I was coming up on a disturbance when I hit somethin'. I jumped out to see a full bird laid out behind the truck. My asshole was sucking buttermilk; let me tell you. I went over to see if I could do anything and was surrounded. One of the rioters, asshole in a Navy shirt too," he jabbed, "came at me. I yelled, he didn't stop, so I put one in his chest. Suddenly that bird started biting and clawing at me, growling like a dog, and the other guy got back up. And that's when I figured it out."

"What?" Rob asked as he reached an intersection. Dillingham pointed to keep going straight.

"That to kill these things, they ain't people anymore that's for damn sure, you gotta shoot the bastards in the head."

Rob nodded his head. "Yeah, I found that out too on the way here. Any idea what they are?"

"Damned if I know. But I'll tell you what; I fought my way through that mob, putting those bastards down. It seemed like every time I killed one, two more took its place. I dropped as many as I could, but they kept comin', growling and grabbin' at me the whole way. Came damn close to eatin' it a few times, and one even tried to take a chunk out of my chest, but got a mouthful of Kevlar instead. So I looked for somewhere to hold out until I could get on the radio. I found that utility shed and hid my ass in there, those bastards growling and banging on the walls until they lost interest I guess. Then tried to get a hold of somebody on the radio or my cell phone, but nothing worked and eventually I had to piss like a race horse, which is when you found me."

Rob's mind grabbed onto the last comment. "Dillingham! Do you still have your phone?"

"Well sure," he said pulling the phone off the clip on his belt, "it ain't gonna do you a damn bit of good though. I haven't been able to reach nobody on that thing since the explosion." He handed the phone over.

Rob took it and slowed the vehicle next to a large brick building. "Thank you!" he said under his breath, examining the phone. It was one of the new smartphones that had more processing power than his computer in college.

On the bottom of the large backlit screen, a WiFi icon could be seen. Quickly scrolling through the different programs, Rob found the instant messaging application and logged in. Selecting Sarah's name, he typed, "Are you there?" Seconds ticked by, then the phone made a soft mewling noise.

Sarah's response flashed on the screen. "THNK GOD! WHERE R U!?"

"On Base, Where r u exactly?"

"WE R ON EAST SIDE OF SERVICE RUNWAY. 4 BRICK BLGS. MOST NORTHERN BLDG. PLEASE HURRY ROB!"

"Ok, I'll be there soon. Listen for us. Do you know how many THINGS R around you?"

"BEEN QUIET. DUNNO. PLZ HURRY!"

Rob dropped the cell into his lap. "We need to get to the service runway. How do we get there?"

Dillingham again pointed ahead. "Keep going, this will lead out to the main runway, and then we can cut over."

A sad looking little girl had shambled into the glow of the headlights, its face twisted into a hateful sneer and uttering a high pitch growl as it charged the Blazer. Rob smashed the accelerator, ramming the girl with a loud pop as the child's face imploded from the force of the blow, and drove toward the runway.

The ten foot tall chain link security gate sat partially agape as the Blazer approached. "Hold on!" Rob said enthusiastically as he rammed the gate, sending a shower of sparks over the concrete. The night seemed eerily quiet as they pulled onto the runway. Only one hulking C-130 cargo aircraft could be seen in its taxi landing lights that sent their silent beacons into the still darkness. Several aircraft support vehicles sat motionless with no operators to move them. The runway itself was clear, and if not for the lack of personnel, looked like the fully operational airport that it was.

"Keep to your left-- that will get you onto the service runway." Dillingham advised as he instinctively surveyed the deserted airstrip for any threats. The service runway was obscured by several large hangers, and as the Blazer made the wide turn, a Gulfstream V came into view. Government markings on the tail of the small swept-wing aircraft could barely be seen in the light of the hanger's security lights. Scorch marks were clearly visible on the left side of the aircraft, seeming to emanate from the left turbine. Two piles of charred debris, the larger directly below the engine, the other strewn behind it, littered the concrete. The bulkhead door of the plane was opened and integral stairs had been extended to the tarmac. While this didn't seem odd, the normalcy ended as Rob's eyes tracked to the ground below. A large pool of blood, looking jet black in the darkness of the night, covered the area around the stairs. Pools of blood were beginning to be the theme of the evening, he thought darkly. Several men in the dark suits that seemed to be the uniform for every bureaucrat in Washington lay in distorted positions in the pools, staining their expensive clothing. Several yards away the two members of the flight crew could be seen lying face down on the tarmac, weapons scattered a few feet away. The wounds on the bodies seemed random. Bites and scratches covered almost every inch of their exposed flesh from their extremities to areas where clothes had been torn and skin exposed. The killing blow looked to be common on all the victims. Large gashes, bites and even areas where flesh seemed to have been torn away could easily be seen on the bodies.

Slowly driving past the carnage, Rob caught sight of several small buildings at the end of the runway. Focused on his goal, he didn't see the body in the green flight suit until clipping it with the front fender and sending it spinning into the night. Snapping their eyes from the scene, both Dillingham and Rob took careful note of their surroundings. From between the buildings to their left, they were able to make out several more bodies in green flight suits or desert cammo moving in the direction of the runway.

"Awww hell." Dillingham said, as he checked the ammo in his M4 and slung the weapon over his right arm.

"Listen, I have an idea. Do you see the light in the left building over there? I am sure that's the one." He said pointing. Dillingham grunted his affirmation. "I am going to pull up at an angle with the back of the truck as close to the building as possible and leave just enough room in the front to get the door open. I figure that will keep any unwanted guests out while I grab Sarah."

"And just how long do you reckon this here task is going to take? I didn't join up with you just to get eaten out on the flight line." Dillingham said as he again surveyed his surroundings and the advancing bodies. Both men paused for a minute, taking in what the sergeant had just said. They looked at each other and let out a guffaw of laughter. That seemed to cut the tension, and each man relaxed slightly.

"In and out, quick and dirty." The glow of the dash caught in Rob's teeth as he flashed the sergeant a goofy grin.

"Let's shit and git then son."

Quickly checking the rearview mirror, Rob could see that the closest body was at least a few hundred yards back. As the Blazer edged in close to the steel building, a sliver of light could be seen behind the single window. A loud scraping and cracking sound of breaking plastic was heard inside of the vehicle as the back end of the SUV contacted the wall, coming to a halt directly parallel to the building's sturdy fire door. Rob opened the Blazer's door, pushing it out with enough force to wedge it ajar, thus effectively blocking that route from any potential threats. Hesitantly, he stepped out of the vehicle, stepping over and grasping the door handle. Rob pounded on the door and called, "Sarah! It's Rob! Open up!" The chrome handle turned with an audible click as the bolt slid aside and the door swung open.

Dillingham turned his attention to the matter at hand, rolling down the window and pointing the stubby barrel of the M4 out the window. The main drawback of the M4 was the shortened barrel. While this was an advantage over the slightly more cumbersome M16 in portability and close quarters combat, the unfortunate side effect was that of a reduced range and accuracy. The sergeant calmly switched off the safety and waited for the things to make their way into his field of fire.

CHAPTER TEN

Standing in the doorway was a small, slender young woman with honey colored shoulder length hair and a freckled nose. She leapt forward, throwing her arms around Rob's midsection and burying her face into his shoulder. "Thank God you made it! I didn't know how else I was going to make it out of here alive!" As Rob started to put his arms out to comfort her, Sarah leaned up giving him a quick but meaningful kiss. Momentarily, but pleasantly taken aback, Sarah grabbed Rob and led him inside the building. The interior of the building looked to be small office space. Several cubicles made up the back of the building, each containing a desk, computer and other typical office accouterments. The front half was decorated as half reception, half recreational area. A small desk and office chair were situated directly to the left of the door behind which a large oak billiards table filled the space. Opposite, several plush couches, overstuffed chairs and a coffee table covered in old sports magazines completed the look.

On the couch was a bespectacled and harried looking man clutching a brief case. Sarah grabbed Rob's hand and led him over to the couch. "Rob, this is Chad Leske—."

Rob cut her off. "Hello Chad. We need to cut it short and get the hell out of here. There are a ton of those things out there headed our way. Follow me." With that, he headed toward the door just as a loud clack-clack-clack echoed in the steel building. "Let's go!" he yelled and sprinted toward to door.

Once the bodies reached about a hundred yards from the Blazer, they were quickly gunned down by the sergeant's skillful shots. Unfortunately, the bodies kept coming in greater numbers threatening to overtake the island of survivors. Perception heightened by the danger, Dillingham made out the footsteps behind him. "Get your asses in here now! We need to git while the gittin's good!" Rob could see the bodies approaching through the windows of the Blazer and yanked open the back door.

"Get in!' He yelled behind him. Sarah quickly climbed into the vehicle followed by Chad, slamming the door behind him. Rob got back behind the wheel, quickly pulling away. The door dislodged from the building, the truck's motion forcing the door closed.

The Blazer cut a sharp right turn heading back toward the main runway. The wheels squealed as the bulky SUV weaved between the approaching bodies. Occasionally, bodies would glance off the sides of the body, causing Sarah and Chad to jump in their seats. As he reached the main runway, Rob made another sharp right turn toward the airfield security gates. In the lights of the Blazer, several bodies could be seen in the gap of the gates. Rob hesitated, slowing the vehicle's forward momentum. "Go!" cried the sergeant as he slapped the dashboard twice. Depressing the accelerator, the SUV bared down on the now approaching bodies. The first two bodies growled as they each hit a fender. Sarah saw one pass by her window. The legs of the thing were bent forward at an unnatural angle. It growled and reached out for the passing vehicle just before it sped into the night. A second later, a bump followed by a large crunch made everyone cringe. The front of the vehicle hit the body squarely in the center of the hood. The force of the blow caused the body to fly into the windshield, causing it to bow in as cracks formed from the center of impact. A large crimson stain began to run down the center of the windshield as thankfully the speed of the moving vehicle caused the body to roll off the top of the Blazer.

Rob had to lean slightly to the left to see out of the shattered windshield and was hit with a sudden realization. What do we do now? He was so focused on just getting to Sarah that he had no idea what to do next. As they reached the main thoroughfare of the base, no bodies could be seen in the immediate area. Rob slowed the vehicle to a stop and turned to look at his passengers. Before Dillingham could question him yet again he said, "Okay ya'll, what do we do now."

"Whatcha mean by that?" the sergeant said, obviously irritated by their lack of motion.

"Ummm, so, uhhh, yeah..." Rob drawled. "I had a great plan up until I came and got Sarah. After that, things get a little fuzzy. I didn't quite plan that far ahead."

"Where were you on that one, dipshit," Dillingham said mockingly.

"Knock it off!" Sarah yelled then composed herself before continuing. "Okay, so where should we go? There has to be help somewhere. Have you guys heard anything on the radio?"

"Hoo-lee shit, Sergeant Anderson! I thought you were done for sure. In fact, I was coming out to help you pull your head out of your ass." Dillingham said, turning to face the young woman. "Although, I do have to admit no self-respecting SF would cry to a squid for help." The man's face darkened. "Mendez?"

"She was bitten when we were attempting to clear the hospital." Sarah's eyes watered slightly. "I got her out, but she attacked me later and…"

"I understand, Sergeant. You did what you had to." Dillingham replied softly, turning to Rob. "So what have you heard?"

"I have been listening all night until I wrecked the Jeep--Long story. From what I heard, these things are everywhere."

"Then obviously, we need to get away. Just get out of town or something like that—" Sarah began.

"That is going to be very difficult. But I agree we need to get out of the area, preferably by six this morning." Chad interrupted from the back.

"Why is that?" Rob asked incredulously.

"Well, that is when several submarine launched ballistic missiles will hit the city of Tampa." Chad said nonchalantly. "This will neutralize the threat of further contamination."

"They ain't never gonna drop a bomb on an American city. There ain't no way they'd get away with it?" Dillingham chimed in.

"Believe it. They will just blame it on extremists. A terrorist plot to demoralize the population by killing all the emergency personnel, FEMA, DHS, even the National Guard with a second attack," he giggled, "of course none of those agencies are *actually* in the area. Nope, they were stopped at the quarantine."

"I saw something about that on the news earlier, about the National Guard stopping people from leaving." Looking up into the rearview mirror, Rob saw a figure make its way out of the shadows and picking up pace as it made out the Blazer. "Here comes company." he said, pulling away.

"Don't worry too much. We are safe in here as long as we keep moving. They can't move very fast." Chad deadpanned as he concentrated on the briefcase in his lap.

"Sarah, who is this guy?" Rob asked.

She slid over a bit closer to the door. I don't know. He didn't say much. I just asked his name and told him that help was on the way." Her eyes fell on Rob in the driver's seat.

"Oh, don't worry. In fact, I may be your best asset." Chad said playfully.

This guy has lost it, Rob thought, exasperated. Then asked, "Alright, enough of this. What are you talking about?"

"Should I start at the beginning?"

Rob looked up and stared at the man in the rearview mirror, watching him twitch and giggle while he stroked the briefcase in his lap. The most unnerving quality of the man was the thousand-yard stare that the man had adopted.

Great, he thought, exactly what I need right now, some lunatic with a god complex. Diverting his attention back the road ahead, he could see the main gate quickly approaching. A large car, maybe a Cadillac or Lincoln, had tried to run the gate on the right side. From the scrapes on the cement barricade, the vehicle must have clipped them before heading for the cinderblock wall framing the gate. As the Blazer turned, the extent of the damage to the gate became clear. If not for the crumpled mass of metal barely visible on the other side of hole, it would be easy to believe that an explosive charge had been used to breach the wall. An almost perfect half circle had been knocked out, giving Rob the opportunity to escape.

He nosed the truck toward the hole. Everyone let out a startled cry when the SUV bucked up and down like a bronco, bouncing over the broken cinder blocks. As the vehicle began edging through the hole, screeching could be heard from the undercarriage and Rob realized he had just made a huge mistake. Concrete itself is a very sturdy building material under the force of compression. But tension placed on the same horizontal concrete structure will cause it to fail more easily. In order to overcome this weakness, steel reinforced bars are used in construction to steady concrete structures to this tensile stress. He cringed as he thought of the exposed steel ripping the tires to shreds like a cheese grater. With a final bump, the rear of the Blazer cleared the last of the damaged wall. Picking up speed and heading out onto the empty boulevard, Rob waited for the telltale whump-whump-whump of a flattened tire. Hearing none, he exhaled a sigh of relief. Looking up to catch sight of Chad in the rearview mirror but instead saw Sarah's blue eyes staring back at him. The obvious fear of the situation could easily be seen in that look, but also consternation. Hazarding a glance to the right, Dillingham stared out the window into the night. Ever vigilant, his eyes swept back and forth through his periphery looking for threats.

Rob bit his lip while he thought. A sad-sounding giggle came from the back seat and solidified the first order of business in his mind. I have to get somewhere safe and find out what this guy is talking about. He slowed and began looking closer at the buildings as they passed. Pawnbrokers, money-lending businesses and your typical fast food joints lined the road that led away from the base. Rob recognized these but also knew that often one more feature surrounded military bases: cheap apartments and housing developments. Crossing through an intersection, the traffic signal only monotonously blinking its red light, a small subdivision could be seen on the right. Signaling, a moot point with the lack of traffic but a habit nonetheless, Rob turned the vehicle down the quiet neighborhood streets. He was looking for something specific and did not have to wait long.

As the Blazer rounded the first corner, a family of four was loading up a large grey Ford SUV the size of a small bus. The mother looked to be helping a small child belt in the back while an older boy ran around and climbed in on the driver's side. The father-keeping sentry with a large hunting rifle swung around at the sound of the approaching vehicle. Rob watched as the man tracked the vehicle with the rifle while his wife got into the passenger side. As the Blazer rolled on, Dillingham looked into the side mirror just in time to see the man get into the driver's side.

After circling almost the entire subdivision, Rob finally found what he was looking for. On the left a ranch-style house, sat dark with no lights illuminating the interior of the home. An attached two-car garage sat with its door open like a gaping maw. Swinging the vehicle into the driveway and turning on the bright beams of the headlights, he peered into the garage. There was no movement that he could see and no bodies lurking in the shadows. "Get out and shut that garage door," he said to Dillingham as he pulled slowly into the garage.

Dillingham set the M4 against the dash, pulled out his M9 and cautiously opened the door. A small beacon of light was visible on the wall as he made his way around the Blazer. As he got closer, Dillingham recognized the small rectangle as the garage door control button and slapped it with the palm of his hand. A squeal of metal followed by the hum of machinery filled the garage as the door began to move. After what seemed like an eternity, the door closed with a metallic clang. Dillingham then flipped the switch for the garage light and again visually checked the garage. "All clear," he said sitting down on the cement stair leading into the house. There were several clicks as multiple doors opened, and the occupants spilled out into the garage. Sarah rounded the rear hatch and made her way over next to Dillingham while Rob stepped out and slammed his door.

Turning to look at Chad, he demanded, "Now explain!" Chad made his way to an old wooden chair against the wall its green upholstered back frayed and faded, then sat down.

He stifled a giggle with a clearing of his throat and tried to compose himself. Facing the group he said, "Like I said earlier before circumstances so rudely interrupted me, I will start from the beginning." The other three stared back at him expectantly. His demeanor changed before their eyes. Sitting rigidly with his back straight and feet flat on the floor, he had the look of a professor about to give a lecture, not the Looney Toon that had been giggling in the back seat. "My name is Chad Leske as the young lady mentioned earlier. What you do not know is that I am the assistant to the director of the Centers for Disease Control and Prevention. The earlier explosion at the International Airport has had dire consequences not just for Tampa, but for the United States and potentially the world as well. What I am about to tell you is classified, but since I don't figure we'll make it out of here alive, what the hell."

Rob was about to interrupt the man and ask him just exactly *why* he didn't think they would get out alive, but decided against it. Instead, he leaned against the washing machine behind him and continued listening.

"What happened earlier today, the explosion, was in fact a terrorist attack. It is a terrible tragedy that is not to be overlooked." He paused for a moment, looked down briefly, and continued. "The problem, you see, was beneath the airport: a high security level four bio-medical research facility. I will spare you the details of this facility, but suffice to say they handled some very dangerous organisms. Just one of the many handled there was HTOV, the Human Terminal Operability Virus. Its purpose was to allow terminally wounded casualties to continue to fight by preventing shock, blocking pain receptors, and quickly clotting the blood."

"What's that got to do with what's goin' on right now?" Dillingham asked, getting noticeably agitated at the length of the explanation. He had always said skip the delivery and gimme the baby, and this delivery was taking way too long.

Chad took off his glasses and began using his tie to nervously clean them. "Unfortunately, during development there were some unexpected, umm, effects. Each time researchers tested on animals, the virus never actually worked as predicted and the test animals would just die after being infected. Several tests concluded that shortly after the death of the test subjects, they would begin moving again as if alive. The initial theory was electrical discharge in the brain causing the movement. This was eventually discounted when further tests proved that the subjects would react to outside stimulus."

Sarah looked at Chad, disbelief spreading across her face. Frowning she said, "What do you mean by 'outside stimulus'?"

"I mean they reacted to the world around them. They would bite, scratch and struggle even though they were clinically dead. When the results of the testing were reported, the powers that be were thrilled. The research was a failure in one respect, but think of the possibilities if the virus' effects could be controlled!" Chad exclaimed.

"Bullshit." Dillingham spat.

"So, I get that these people are infected by something, and from what I've seen so far it sounds a lot like this 'HT'-whatever virus. But dead… like what, *zombies*?" Rob asked incredulously.

"Sir that is exactly what I am saying."

The palpable silence that followed filled the stuffy garage as the group simply stared at Chad. The click of the air conditioner coming to life from outside startled everyone back into the moment.

"Bullshit." Dillingham reiterated.

Sarah turned to Dillingham. "Sergeant please, let's hear him out." The group again turned their attention to the man in the chair.

"As you can imagine, the spread of this virus would be catastrophic. There is a contingency plan in place to control an outbreak. First attempt will be to contain the outbreak through quarantine and destroying the infected. Additionally, high level government and military officials in the area are to be immunized."

"Wait, there is an immunization?" Rob asked excitedly.

"Certainly!" Chad's face perked up as he tapped the case. "In fact, I have it right here. But again, the point is moot."

"No it's not!" Sarah said as she lept to her feet. "You have the immunization! You can make sure we don't get infected!"

Chad's face fell. "Unfortunately the first attempt has failed. My colleagues and I were attacked, and I am the only one left—"

"But that's enough!" Sarah interrupted. "We can make it out of here!"

Irritably Chad replied, "As I was saying, I am the only one left. All my colleges were killed on our arrival thus rendering the mission impo—"

"You have the immunization?" Sarah asked nervously. "That is all we need!"

Anger flashed across Chad's face after being interrupted yet again. Looking as though he were about to yell, his features quickly softened again into a serene mask.

"Unfortunately my dear, that is not how they will see it. When we failed to report in after landing, the mission defaulted to the second option: Destruction of the threat. At 5:50 this morning, three submarine launched intercontinental ballistic missiles will be fired toward Tampa. By six, there will be nothing left. This will neutralize the threat and sanitize the area."

Sarah uttered a frightened whisper, "Oh—my—God."

"Damn," Rob croaked and cleared his throat. "We have to get the hell out of here and fast." He glanced at his watch. "Right now it's 3:30. That gives us two and a half hours to get far enough away from the blast. Any suggestions?"

"Why don't we just drive away?" Sarah inquired.

"Can't," Rob replied, "like he said, the area is quarantined. Like I said before, they were running a story on it earlier."

"But they can't just leave guardsmen out there to die while enforcing the quarantine?"

"Martyrs to the cause," Chad said, giggling as his demeanor slipped. "They will get a holiday named after them."

Dillingham, who had adopted a thousand yard stare, jerked himself back to reality. "How 'bout a boat?"

"Huh?" Rob said turning.

"A boat. We can just take one from one of the marinas."

"Nope!" Chad said in a sing-song voice, "They quarantine the water too!"

"There can't be that many ships in the area. There's no naval base for a couple hundred miles, Key West I think. It takes a long tong time to get ships into position, a lot longer than just a few hours. I think all we have to worry about is Coast Guard Helicopters, and they won't risk damaging those in the blast to come after us…at least I hope not." Rob looked at Dillingham, "What do you have in mind?"

"I go fishin' all the time out off Gandy Park, and they've got one of those high-end marinas out there with whatever you need. I figure we get us something fast, like a Donzi."

"Alright," Rob said, confidence filling his voice, "here's the plan. We're going to make a run for the marina. With everyone leaving so quickly I am sure we will be able to get something out of there. From there I figure we can head south toward Sarasota or Naples where can try to disappear. " He looked around to everyone, staring them straight in the eyes. "But, if anyone has a better idea, I am open to suggestions." No one spoke but Chad, who giggled to himself on his chair while rocking back and forth.

"Hey Rob," Sarah said as she pushed away from the wall where she was leaning, "I think we should get some supplies. Maybe see if there is some bottled water or fruit in the house?" She pointed in the direction of the door.

Rob was about to object, but held his tongue. They may have to lie low for a few days if they run into anything while trying to escape. "Good idea. Go check out the kitchen and see if you can find anything we might need." Sarah gave a thumbs-up and stepped past Dillingham to the door. Turning the handle, the door opened easily and she slid her way into the quiet darkness. He turned his attention back to Chad, who was now muttering something incoherent to himself. "Chad." Rob bent over and snapped his fingers in front of the man's face. "Chad! You with me?"

Chad jerked out of his reverie and looked up at Rob with fear in his eyes. "Wha-what?" he stuttered.

"Hey buddy, I need you to keep it together okay? If we're gonna make it through this we need everybody's help." He swung his arm up to place it on Chad's shoulder and the man flinched. Rob lowered his arm. "Can you hang in there until we get out of this?"

"I think so," he said sheepishly.

"Great," Rob said calmly, "I need you to get those immunizations ready for us. I don't want to risk anyone getting bit and turning into one of those things."

"Zombies!" Chad jumped in emphatically.

"Whatever the hell they are. Can you do that for us?"

Chad straightened up, stiffening his resolve as he was filled with a new purpose. "Certainly." he replied, snapping open the locks on the briefcase and lifting the lid. The interior of the case was lined in thick, dark foam with cutouts to hold various items. Chad picked up a glass vial and looked at it closely. Apparently satisfied with the contents, he set it back down. He then pulled out several plastic wrapped syringes, lining them up in a row and pulling the plastic off the first.

Rob, satisfied with the man's progress, turned his attention back to Dillingham. The sergeant was taking a closer look at the front of the Blazer and inspecting the damage from their earlier flight. "Hey Rob, say, can you pop the hood for me? I want take a closer look at the radiator." Dillingham asked as he hunkered down on his knees to take a look under the front of the vehicle.

"I gotcha," Rob replied as he opened the car door. Bending down he found the hood release, pulling it and opening the hood with a clunk. Starting to stand back up, a strangled cry rang out. Leaping up in response, his head again smacked the doorframe and bright spots filled his vision. "Shit! Again!" He cursed, quickly stumbling to the door.

The interior of the house was pitch black except for a small incandescent nightlight. Giving off a meager glow, it barely illuminated the hallway that ran the length of the house. A couch could be seen backlit by the open door as well as a dining room table off to the right. In the silence of the house, stifled breathing could be heard in the murky dark beyond the table. Rob reached down to his hip, pulling out the Barretta and switching off the safety. Chancing a quick glance over his shoulder he looked for Dillingham, who was nowhere to be seen.

"Little help!" he called and slowly began to make his way through the house, pistol at the ready. As Rob's eyes began to adjust to the darkness, the silhouettes of two figures could be seen by the large bay window in the kitchen.

"That's far enough," a gruff voice with a slight accent said as Rob rounded the table, "drop the gun!"

"Hey, if this is your house we aren't here to rob you. We just needed to get away—."

"Shut the fuck up," the figure yelled, "and drop your damn gun!" Rob could see now that the man had a pistol of his own and was pointing it in his direction as well. At that moment, the smaller figure began to struggle against the larger figure. In the dim light Rob could see the larger figure grab a tighter hold on the smaller, causing her to let out a squeak.

"All right, I am putting my gun down. Just let her go." Rob leaned over and set the Barretta on the table.

The larger figure gave a derisive snort under his breath. He made a move to lower the pistol toward the smaller figure. Light suddenly flooded the room. Rob, momentarily blinded, stumbled into the dining room table as he reached for his gun. A split second later, a deafening crack originating from the direction of the garage, filled the large room. Rob's ears rang with the sudden trauma of the gunshot, and as his vision clarified, he saw Dillingham crossing the room. Sarah was kicking and scratching her way from behind the island in the kitchen, blood covering the right side of her green ABUs. Rob could see that she was yelling something but it was indistinguishable in his ringing ears. He deftly grabbed the 9mm from the oak tabletop and started toward Dillingham. The was a bright muzzle flash and another muffled bang as Dillingham put another round into the figure on the ground.

Rob ran over and met Sarah halfway as she started to get to her feet. She collapsed against him, and he could feel her wracking sobs as she pressed her face into his t-shirt. In the kitchen, Dillingham was stepping away from the figure on the floor. It looked to be a man in his early twenties with dark tan skin. The white pullover he was wearing was stained with red, blood flowing from a gunshot wound in the right side of the man's chest. In the grout between the beige tiles on the floor, small crimson rivers formed, split and merged as the attacker bled out.

As the ringing in Rob's ears began to fade, he heard a final sniffle as Sarah regained her composure. She looked at him with bleary, red eyes then turned and sprinted over to Dillingham. Throwing her arms around the sergeant in a bear hug, she cried, "Thank you! I thought I was dead."

Dillingham was slightly taken aback, but allowed the smallest flicker of a smile as he looked down at the woman. "No problem. You would have done the same." he said, patting Sarah on the back. She released her grip on the man.

"Nice shooting man!" Rob exclaimed and looked down at the body. Pointing with a flick of his head he asked, "What the hell was that all about?"

"Bastard! I was almost to the kitchen when he reached out from behind me. He put me in a chokehold so I couldn't scream and told me if I made a sound I was dead." She walked over and kicked the body with the toe of her boot. "Asshole." she said and spat on the dead body.

"I was afraid of this." Dillingham added to the conversation. "We are going to have to be more careful. With all the Johnny Laws busy fightin' the Zombies, assholes are going to be out in force tryin' to take advantage."

Rob hadn't even thought of that. Christ, he thought, I have been so preoccupied with the zombies... He cringed, that would take some getting used to…zombies. Suddenly, Chad and the inoculation came to mind. Sprinting over to the doorway, he could see him sitting serenely in his chair, filling another syringe from a glass vial. "Hey, you okay?" Rob asked.

"Of course! The inoculations are ready when you are." Chad replied as he put down the last syringe, not showing any sign of concern over the commotion in the other room.

Rob shook his head, turned and headed back into the other room. Looking at Sarah he asked, "So you're alright?"

"Yes, I'm fine. Let's grab what we need and get out of here." she said as she opened a cabinet to her right. Dillingham, following her lead, opened the pantry and started searching its contents. Rob noticed a large red backpack, obviously owned by some teenager due to the various band names and graffiti, on the sofa. Across the room, Dillingham had found a stash of snacks: various energy bars, fruit snacks and pudding cups, which he laid on the island. Sarah, finding only dishes and kitchen appliances in the upper cabinets, bent down to look in a lower cabinet. "Bingo!" she said excitedly, pulling half a case of water out of the cabinet and hefting it onto the counter. Rob hurried over with his find, opening the bag and beginning to fill it with water bottles. Once the plastic wrapped case of water was emptied, he began haphazardly throwing snacks into the bag.

Dillingham and Sarah had about finished ransacking the kitchen when the sergeant yelled, "Yo Rob, catch!" A small metal object flew the short distance between the men, landing in the palm of Rob's hand. Looking down, he saw that it was a bottle opener emblazoned with a pink flamingo. "You never know when you are going to need one of those." Dillingham said as he slid the drawer closed and stepped over the dead man as he made his way into the dining room. Red tread marks left by the boots were a grim reminder of what had just happened.

Sarah closed the last cabinet and turned to Rob. "Let's get out of here. I have had enough fun for one night." She gave Rob a sad little smile as she walked around him toward the garage door. Zipping up the backpack and swinging it over his shoulder, Rob followed.

The musty smell of the gasoline and lawn clippings met them as they stepped back into the garage. Rob pulled the door closed behind him. This would at least slow down any more unpleasant surprises, hopefully giving them a few precious seconds to react. Chad ripped open a small square alcohol swab, saying, "Okay, first person please." Rob motioned to Sarah to go first, chivalry getting the better of him. That is what he kept telling himself as he eyed Chad warily. "Please pull your sleeve up to your shoulder." She quickly her arm out of the ABU blouse and wrinkled her nose as he cleaned the area just below her shoulder with the alcohol swab. Picking up the first syringe and gently uncapping it, he said, "Now, you will feel a slight pinch at first, but the injection itself is very…. unpleasant." Before she could react, Chad plunged the needle into her arm. Initially, there was only a slight pinch, no different than any other shot she had gotten. Then suddenly, Sarah's arm felt like it was on fire.

"Ahhhh," she growled, clenching her teeth. Chad, finishing the injection, quickly pulled the needle out. A small drop of blood formed at the injection site and dropped to the floor as Sarah swung her arm in a circle trying to relieve the pain. "Okay, that sucked." she said, massaging the arm.

"Yes, I am afraid it is not a pleasant experience to be sure." Chad remarked, then formally, "Next please." Dillingham looked at Rob who gave him a nod to go first. The sergeant walked over and rolled up his sleeve for the injection. He did not flinch as the injection pierced his skin or as Chad depressed the plunger. When finished, he simply rolled down his sleeve and stepped aside. Rob suddenly broke out in a cold sweat. Ever since he was a small child he had hated needles. In fact, until he was about twelve, it would take his parents and several nurses to pin him down to give him one. Even as he got older, he would clench his muscles so tight that he would pass out. After joining the Navy, the proverbial "suck it up" was ingrained into him, but that still didn't make him enjoy it. Forcing back the feelings, he slowly stepped forward and pulled up his shirtsleeve. Chad, noticing his nervousness, said calmly, "It'll be over before you know it." Rob jumped slightly as the needle broke the skin. “Please relax,” Chad said more firmly. As the liquid entered his arm, Rob was reminded of red ant bites. Thousands and thousands of red ant bites spreading down his arm.

“Damn.” he said under his breath, fresh sweat breaking out on his brow. Chad removed the needle and Rob began massaging his arm. “Well, that was fun,” he said sarcastically. Turning, he opened the door of the Blazer and tossed the backpack inside. He could hear the sound of the case snapping closed and turned back to Chad. “What are you doing? You need one too?” Rob said, pointing to the case.

“Do you honestly think we would have been sent here by the President without already receiving the shot?” Chad replied incredulously as he stood up.

Looking at his watch, Rob noted the time: 4:37. “It’s time to get out of here ya’ll.” he said, walking toward the driver’s door. “We’ve only got about an hour and a half and it’s a ways to Hookers point.” Dillingham rounded the front of the Blazer, slamming the hood closed while Sarah and Chad climbed into the back seat. The engine hesitated slightly as the key twisted in the ignition, but after some gentle feathering of the gas pedal it roared to life. Looking in the rearview mirror, Rob realized he had forgotten to open the garage door. Getting out, he ran over to press the illuminated button and the door began to open with a metallic groan as he got back in the Blazer.

The white backup lamps of the Blazer flashed to life as the transmission went into reverse. The garage door rose the final few feet to a wall of figures filling the rear window. Several zombies lunged toward the vehicle, mindlessly hitting their heads on the door as they tried to capture their prey. "Hold on, this is going to get bumpy!" Rob called as he stomped on the accelerator.

The SUV slammed into the wall of bodies, felling them like cornstalks under a combine. Half way out, the wheels lost traction, spinning uncontrollably and splashing gore across the side of the Blazer. Rob let off the gas for a moment and slammed the transmission into neutral. Zombies were surrounding the Blazer, growling in unison and slamming their limbs into the cab. Rob hit the button for four-wheel drive just as a fat, blood-covered teenager shattered his forearm by slamming it into the window pillar. He watched fascinated as the creature continued its assault until the arm split and bone clacked against the window with each thrust. "Go!" Sarah screamed from the backseat and he placed the Blazer into gear. The three unencumbered wheels caught purchase, pulling them free of the mob and into the suburban street. Blood covered wheels screeched to a halt as the truck changed direction, roaring off into the night to escape the subdivision.

The creatures however came from every direction in vain attempts to stop the SUV. Occasionally, one would come close enough to scratch the sides, growling angrily at the occupants. At one point what was once a young woman in pink running shorts and yellow tank top managed to get close enough to the front of the Blazer to grab at the windshield with bloody hands. Leaving bloody streaks on the already shattered windshield, she was rewarded with several shattered ribs from the mirror as it disintegrated from colliding with her midsection.

Rob reached the subdivision's entrance and headed north. As he drove away from the carnage, the creatures began to thin. The constant barrage of just a few minutes ago became a trickle. About every block or so, a couple could be seen beating on the doors or windows of a house with lights on, people inside attracting their murderous attention until distracted by the noise of the moving vehicle.

CHAPTER ELEVEN

Dillingham inspected his rifle, pulling out the magazine and counting the rounds. "Damn," he said to himself.

"What's up?" Rob asked, leaning over to the left to get a better view of the upcoming intersection out of the shattered window.

"I have all of fifteen rounds left in this magazine." He looked back to Sarah and pointed to the rifle leaning on the seat. "Check that for me." Sarah picked it up, dropped the magazine, and quickly began counting rounds.

"Twenty and," she checked the breech, "one in the chamber."

"I've got a magazine on this web gear." Rob said as he distractedly pulled it out and tossed the magazine to the Sergeant. "And I still have two for the Barretta."

Dillingham pulled his M9 to check the magazine. "Okay, that makes seventy rounds for the nine plus whatever is in yours." Pausing he said," That's no arsenal."

"It's better than nothing." Rob said as he slowed the Blazer to a crawl to approach what was normally a busy intersection at all hours. The traffic lights were out, and he searched the connecting roads. In his limited view, no traffic could be seen in either direction. He slowly made the turn onto Gandy, picking up speed as they passed under the large overpass.

Chad suddenly caught a fit of giggles and blurted out, "As long as you save four for us, we should be fine."

Before anyone could respond, Sarah reached over, grabbed the man by the lapels of his rumpled suit and yanked him toward her. "I have had enough of your shit! Any time you want to get out and walk, be my guest!" She screamed at the man before pushing him back into his seat. Chad looked stunned, blinked and was overcome with another wave of giggles. Sarah, trying to maintain her self-control, turned to look disgustedly out the window.

Dark rows of storefronts and car dealerships filled the landscape. The monotony was broken up by the occasional figure listlessly walking through the night until the sound of the Blazer attracted their presence. They looked so lost and alone, she thought and could almost take pity on them. Until earlier today, they had been working or spending time with their families. Now, she shuddered, their families and friends were under attack, by them.

Up ahead, dual beams of light were racing through the night followed by the throaty roar of V8 engine. Rob erring on the side of safety, brought the Blazer to a halt about a hundred yards from the next intersection. The lights spun to face head on with the SUV. Squeals of tires followed by the whoops and hollers of revelry could be heard over the engine. "What the hell is that?" Dillingham asked, staring into the windshield. The lights began to bear down on the Blazer and materialized into the headlamps of a large red Ford pickup. Several figures caught in the crossing beams of the headlights were moving to attack the large truck. Two men could be seen hanging on to the light bar on the roof as the vehicle bore down on the would-be attackers. Swerving to the left, the driver avoided hitting a swiftly moving creature in ripped blue jeans.

A shrill, "Yeeehaaaaw!" carried over the roar of the engine as a large man with a protruding gut leaned over the side of the pickup with a baseball bat. The squishy sound of a melon smashing to the pavement followed, as the head of a zombie exploded, and the body fell harmlessly to the ground. "Yeah buddy!" The man beside him cried and slapped the large man on the back. The driver joined in the cries and shoved his arm out the window waving it in victory. The brush guard knocked down two more figures as they approached the truck and crushed them under the wheels of the large Ford. Swinging back to the right, the second figure lined up on an older woman in a blood speckled yellow dress, growling and reaching for him. He swung the golf club, a large wood by the size of the head, connecting with the side of the old woman's face and spraying gore onto the street. The truck mowed down three more creatures before it was fully illuminated by the Blazers headlights. Dillingham could see that the revelers were three men in their early 20's, each holding a beer can in hand and drunker than a skunk.

"What the hell do they think they are doing?" Rob asked astonished. The truck started forward, swerving out of the path of the pickup.

"Get some!" the fat man screamed, swinging back the arm holding the beer. Just as the front of the truck passed front of the Blazer, the man heaved the beer with a grunt. The silver projectile found its mark on the side window behind Sarah. The window exploded as the can hit, causing glass and beer to spray the rear of the Blazer in a fan.

Sarah and Chad screamed in shock as they were peppered with broken safety glass and foamy beer. The vehicle slid to the sudden stop across the vacant roadway, stopping just shy of two bodies lying still on the pavement. Dillingham had the window down before they had even stopped. Lifting the rifle, he took close aim at the retreating truck. The rear tires could be seen easily in the glow of the red taillights. Quickly taking aim and releasing his breath, Dillingham fired off two rounds. Two pops followed by loud hissing rewarded the marksman. The truck skidded, fishtailed wildly into a brick retaining wall and rolled over on its side. The two men in the back were ejected, rolling and bouncing another 50 feet into the empty parking lot. The Ford rolled onto its crumpled top, rocking back and forth slowly.

Whipping around Rob asked, "Are you okay?"

"Yeah, I think so." Sarah said panting, wiping beer out of her face and shaking glass out of her hair. "What did those idiots think they were doing?"

"Nothing now." Dillingham deadpanned staring out the side windows. He watched as several figures surrounded the two men in the parking lot. Excited growls followed by panicked screams were heard, as the men were gang piled by the zombie mob. The heavyset man's leg was torn away, looking like a large ham, and two creatures fought for the prize like dogs. Observing enough of his handiwork, he said, "Let's go."

Between cracks in the blood-covered windshield, Rob could see zombies starting to swarm in the headlights, drawn by the death cries. "Right," he replied taking his foot off the brake, swerving around two mutilated fast food workers and heading west.

Rob drove cautiously as he covered the remaining two miles to the marina. The lack of light was extremely unnerving and he could not remember ever seeing it this dark his entire life. Even after the hurricanes a few years ago, there had been people's portable generators and battery powered lights, he thought. The lull in activity and lack of sleep were starting to take its toll. Everyone's vision began to blur and eyelids were threatening to close. The bright lights of a radio station ahead transfixed Rob. Apparently, they were running on a generator. In his distraction, he did not notice the Dodge Magnum abandoned in the road ahead. "Look out!" Sarah screamed, diverting his attention and he swerved to narrowly avoid the obstacle. The occasional car notwithstanding, the threat seemed very low in this area, despite being surrounded by residential areas. A yellow sign warning, "Long Bridge ahead – Check Gas" passed over the Blazer as they neared the marina.

"Turn here Rob," the sergeant said as he pointed, "If you take your second right that should bring us right there." Dillingham seemed to have perked up, finally seeing the light at the end of the tunnel. Ignoring the signs for picnic areas and county parks to the right, they continued heading straight. Rob was keeping a keen eye for the turn, and taking in the blackness of Old Tampa Bay. Tearing his eyes away, he caught sight of the garish sign for the Palmetto Yacht Club. "That's it!" Dillingham said, rifle gently bouncing up and down as his leg twitched unconsciously in excitement.

"We might just get out of this alive." Chad chortled from the backseat, but even his voice seemed to lift with a glimmer of hope.

There was no movement as they turned onto the narrow two-lane road. Several boats in various states of repair sat on trailers lining the road, their orange "For Sale" signs glowing as they passed. Sarah and Chad sat forward in their seats, each straining a different direction to get a view out of the destroyed windshield. Rob could see a large sign of light colored granite ahead on the left and as he approached he saw the Palmetto Yacht Club written in large letters. "Here it is!" he exclaimed pulling into the parking lot.

With the exception of several small boats on trailers parked in outside dry slips, the palm tree lined parking lot was empty. A large warehouse, presumably where they stored the various pleasure crafts, loomed to the left while the clubhouse stood directly in front. Rob pulled into a handicapped parking space in front of the club, next to a rope lined path that led into the night and left the Blazer's lights on. "Alright everyone, time to go," he said as he opened the door. Everyone followed suit, Sarah and Dillingham carrying the M4s and Chad clinging to his suitcase. The sky had yet to lighten and the lights of the SUV illuminated the front of the clubhouse in converging circles. Although this ruined their night vision and left the group open to attack from almost any angle, Rob felt it necessary for their preparations. He walked over to the back of the vehicle and picked up the two backpacks. Pulling the red pack over his left shoulder, he walked over to the hood and plunked the other down. Unzipping the black pack, he began to quickly pull items out, sorting them into various piles. "Ah ha!" he said quietly as he pulled a small rubber jacketed flashlight from the bag, turning it on to better illuminate the piles. Water bottles, energy bars and extra magazines were neatly piled on the hood, and he pointed the flashlight inside the black pack, fishing out a sliver multi-tool. Dillingham walked over and picked up one of the magazines.

"I would say you'd been holdin' out on me son," he said as he wiped his hand on his uniform after transferring the clip to the other, "but these things are saltier than a bag a' potato chips."

"They took a bath with me earlier. That is why I didn't mention 'em. But when you started talking about how low on ammo we were, I thought they'd do in a pinch." Rob replied.

"Good enough for government work." Dillingham replied, pocketing half the salty magazines in the cargo pocket of his ABUs.

Sliding off the other backpack, Rob unzipped it and started filling it with the various items splayed out on the hood. Once finished, he pocketed the last remaining clips, zipped up the bag and slung it back over his shoulder. He turned to look at the group. "Dumb question, but does anyone have any idea on how we are going to start the boat when we find one?"

"Don't they usually have these places set up like valet parking?" Sarah asked. "I dated a guy once whos family had a big Bayliner or something down in Naples. They just showed up and their boat was already in the water. All they had to do was see the concierge to get their keys."

"You're right," Rob said with a huff, cursing himself silently for not thinking of it first. "So, they will have the slips numbered. All we have to do is find the one we want and then come back to the club for the keys."

"Sounds like we got ourselves a plan." Dillingham stated. "I reckon that path leads to the water. Rob, you and I take point. You cover the rear." He pointed to Sarah who immediately brought the rifle to bear.

"Roger." Sarah answered, pointing the handgun away, ensuring it was loaded and removing the safety.

"Let's go." Rob stated, transferring the flashlight to his left hand and drawing his M9. The group walked over to the white cement path. Several small white rocks were strewn about the path, no doubt kicked up from the landscaping that lined the walkway. In the beam of the flashlight, the entire breadth of the path was visible, and the group spread out to cover it. The repeated lapping of the waves on the bay were growing louder as the group made their way down toward the water. Several minutes of walking later, the wooden pier was visible in the light and the whispery ghosts of boats could be seen floating in the dark. While the ocean thudded dully under their footsteps, Rob swept the light back and forth on various boats as they passed.

The pier made a sharp right to run parallel with the shoreline and after traveling only a few yards, the sergeant called for them to stop. "Say, let me take a look at this one." Dillingham said, turning. "Hold this," handing the rifle to Rob. Grabbing the flashlight, he pulled the 9mm with his other hand and stepped down onto the boat.

It was a large, luxury speedboat. She had long sweeping lines, about thirty to thirty five feet in length and the lush white seats trimmed in red had room for five. Stepping over to the captain's chair, Dillingham flashed the light over the controls. Brushed chrome surrounded the various gages, a black control panel surrounding the ignition and throttle. Most importantly, the gas gauge read full. Smiling, he stepped down and opened the small door to the cabin. The room contained a built in couch trimmed in the same manner as the seats above, a small galley and what looked to be a head. Dillingham turned around and made his way back topside. "I think she'll do," he said handing the flashlight back over to Rob and stepping out. "Let's go find the key."

Rob swept the light over the deck in front of the vessel, then up one of the pylons to a sign that said Naples. “I don’t see any numbers, so I guess they go by that.” He jerked the light over the sign. “How quaint.”

Dillingham took his rifle back, swinging it over his arm. “I’ll start getting her ready, you go find those keys.” he ordered grabbing the rope and beginning to untie the first cleat.

“I’m on it. Sarah, you stay here and help. Chad, it’s you and me buddy.” Rob grabbed Chad’s coat sleeve and pulled him back toward to club, flashlight lighting the way. Moving quickly down the pier with Chad plodding along slowly behind him, they made their way back to the cement path and up the slope to the club. The glass front doors were still lit by the headlights of the Blazer and Rob tried in vain to pull them open. Not budging. Chad started giggling again, apparently finding humor in the situation. “Shut up.” Rob spat as he made his way to the back of the Blazer. The musty smell of spilled beer permeated the cargo area and fractured glass on the carpet glimmered in the dome light. A tan plastic panel had been shaken loose opening the small storage area. Rob grabbed the panel and pulled it free. Inside sat a small hand jack and, more importantly, a tire iron. Excitedly grabbing the tire iron, Rob ran back to the front doors. He looked over at Chad who was sitting on a cement-parking block a few feet to his left. "You may want to cover your eyes." He then turned and swung the end of the tire iron just to the right of the door handle. A baseball-sized hole was punched into the hurricane glass with a loud crunch. Well that could have gone better, he thought to himself as he hauled back for another swing. This time connecting just slightly above the first hole, he made a slightly larger second hole. The door shook and the sound of glass breaking echoed as blows continued to punch holes around the handle. A minute later, Rob swung one last time to break the last bit of glass around the locking mechanism and used the curved end of the tire iron to pry open the door.

The bleating siren assaulted Rob's ears and emergency floodlights snapped as the door swung open. He jumped back in response, dropping the tool and sending Chad into hysterics. Glowering, Rob bent, picked up his tire iron and stepped into the club.

It was decorated in typical tacky Florida design. Bright pastel green, orange and blues were on display everywhere from the tacky paintings on the walls to the upholstery of the sofas in the lounge. Several large potted trees, fake plastic of course, were dispersed throughout the lobby. Rob looked around and caught sight of a large concierge sign in mirrored script above a desk on the right wall. Stepping around the counter, he found what he was looking for. A cream colored metal box roughly the size of two briefcases, was mounted to the wall beneath the desk.

With precision aim, Rob forced the slotted end of the tire iron in the gap next to the lock. The torque on the tire iron wrenched the cheap stamped metal door from the frame, exposing rows of labeled keys. The steady warble of the alarm was wearing on his nerves as he pointed the flashlight into the box. He started searching franticly, roughly pushing keys around and even knocking some to the floor. Taking a deep breath to calm down, Rob exhaled and concentrated on finding the correct set. In the lower left hand corner, a set of keys with dice on the key ring hung below a peeling, yellowed sticker that read Naples. "Bingo!" Rob cried, snatching the set of keys and taking off towards the door.

A bloodcurdling scream followed by cries for help met him as he reached the broken glass doors. Outside the smoke tinted glass, a horrific scene played out. Several creatures were pinning Chad down, biting, clawing and scratching at the struggling man. Chad let out one more scream that dissolved into a gurgle as a small boy, no more than ten, bit down on the man's Adam's apple. In the light of the Blazer, Rob could see blood spurting from Chad's neck, creating small fans on the pavement. "Christ," he muttered, and looked away. Dark figures were moving quickly through the night toward the club. Damn the alarm, he thought as he tried to think of a way out. I have to go before those other things get here. Rob took a deep breath. "To hell with it!" he yelled, pushing the door open.

The scene played out in slow motion to Rob as he made his escape. Chad, no longer struggling under the barrage from the creatures, lay still on the pavement in a growing pool of his own blood. Two of the zombies looked up at him, their faces and hands looking as though they were dipped in blood. To the right of the carnage, an escape route beaconed, and in it the briefcase lay forgotten. Rob sprinted toward the opening, ignoring the growls of the bloody creatures as he ran. Pausing for a split second to scoop up the case, a clawed hand reached out and caught the cuff of the ABU's. He screamed like a wounded animal, stomping his boot down onto the wrist with a loud crunch. The snapped bones of the creature were unable to maintain a hold on the fabric and released their grip. Two zombies had turned their attention toward the commotion and additional growls could be heard from the parking lot. Rob sprinted toward the path and deftly leapt over the thick rope that lined the cart path. Skidding as he landed on a stray rock, he regained his footing as momentum carried him toward the pier. The loud slap of the boots hitting pavement added an odd syncopation to the growls and howls that followed. Oh great, DJ Zombie Z's greatest hits, Rob thought, finding a moment of humor in his flight.

Reaching the pier he yelled, "Let's go! They're right behind me!"

"You got the keys?" Dillingham called in response as he untied the last line. Sarah leapt into the boat, losing her footing on the landing and stumbling onto the back seat. The sergeant grunted as he fought the lines keeping the boat next to the pier.

Rob rounded the corner and closed the distance to the boat. He thrust the keys at Dillingham, "Let's get the hell out of here, now!" He jumped into the boat and settled into the far bucket seat.

The Sergeant tossed the rifle to Rob. Placing his hands on the hull, he simultaneously kicked the boat away from the dock and lifted himself into the boat. Placing the key in the ignition to the 'ON' position, he pressed the starter button. Dillingham was rewarded with revving then throaty rumble of the large inboard engines starting. "Hot Shit!" he yelled, pushing forward the throttle and flipping on the running lights.

The powerful engines caused large plume of water to spray up as the craft pulled away from the dock. Backlit by the lights of the club, several bodies could be seen moving down the hill toward the water and onto the dock. Rob melted back into the plush seat, allowing himself a sigh of relief for the first time. Straightening up, he glanced down at his watch, which read 5:15. Turning he said over the roar of the engine, "We've got forty-five minutes to get as far away from here as we can. How far do you think we can get?"

Dillingham glanced down at the glowing instrument panel, his eyes searching for the fuel gauge. "These things usually have a range of about 150 miles or so. I figure we can make it to Sarasota or even Naples and then decide what to do from there" he said as the boat cut sharply to port sending Rob's stomach into summersaults and gorge rising into his throat. The irony never escaped him, a sailor who got horribly seasick. Spitting over the side, he looked back to see how Sarah was doing.

"How are you doing back there?" Rob asked over his shoulder.

"I am okay, I guess. I am just trying not to think about anything. I don't know if I should scream or sob my eyes out, so I am just going to try to zone out for a while." she replied over the noise of the engine.

"Sounds like a great idea to me." Rob answered. He was about to turn back when he noticed several lights in the sky. The lights followed a path from east to west, and then seemed to stop dead in the sky. The jostling of the boat over the small waves made observation of the lights difficult and he scrunched his eyes to try to get a better look. Growing larger, the pinpoints of light became floating orbs until they illuminated the sides of a craft in the sky. "Oh, hell" Rob cursed under his breath as the boat was suddenly enveloped in a sheet of blinding white light. Wind buffeted the boat causing it to rock even more and Dillingham was forced to slow to counteract. As their eyes adjusted to the light and the craft slowed, the fiery orange bottle shaped Coast Guard helicopter could be seen hovering above them.

"Attention," a booming voice over the sound of the aircraft's rotors, "you are in violation of the quarantine zone. You are ordered to return to port immediately."

Dillingham switched on the marine radio and punched in channel 16. "Coast Guard Aircraft, this is Technical Sergeant Larry Dillingham, United States Air Force. We are not infected and request escort to the nearest safe port, over." Dillingham said into the radio.

"What are you doing?" Rob asked Dillingham, grabbing his arm. Dillingham shrugged it off as the response came on the radio.

"Sergeant Dillingham, you are ordered to return to port immediately. You are in violation of the quarantine zone. I repeat, return to port immediately, over" came the reply over the boats tinny radio.

"Negative, Coast Guard, we need safe passage to nearest port. We have information vital to command authorities, over."

"Negative Sergeant," the voice broke in over the radio, "you must return to port. This is your final warning. If you do not comply you will be fired upon. I repeat, if you do not turn around we will fire, over."

"Take the wheel!" Dillingham yelled to Rob, shouldering his rifle. "Sarah, get that rifle up, NOW!" Sarah grabbed the rifle, slinging it over her shoulder and aiming at the aircraft.

"Lower your weapons and return to port now! Over" the voice bellowed over the radio.

In the cockpit of the helicopter, another call was coming in over the radio. "Spartan two-one-five, you are clear to engage target, over." the pilot heard in his helmet.

Clicking the mic he replied, "Clear to engage, roger Tampa Guard." He then switched to the internal radio. "Man the 240," he said to the crew in the rear of the aircraft. "Warning shot over the bow."

Rob looked up at the helicopter and saw the side door open. "Oh shit!" he screamed as a barrage of shots harmlessly passed over the bow. "What are we going to do?" Rob yelled at Dillingham, who ignored him.

"Aim for the tail rotor Anderson and fire on my mark." He said calmly to her over the surrounding noise, picking up his M4. Pausing for a moment to aim for a clear shot at the rotors, he exhaled and yelled, "Fire!"

The pop-pop-pop of the three round burst from the M4 rang out, as rounds headed for the aft end of the hovering helicopter. They pelted the tail of the aircraft, punching through the composite skin.

A warning siren sounded in the cockpit as the copilot exclaimed, "Loss of primary hydraulics warning!" The aircraft began to shudder slightly as the pilot struggled to regain control.

"Smoke 'em!" the pilot cried into his mic. The gunner lined up the shot, firing just as a small explosion shook the helicopter.

Sarah watched in horror as the events of the next several seconds played out before her. The rounds from the M4s found their target on the tail of the aircraft. Moments later, a volley of machinegun fire sprayed the deck of the boat, missing her and Rob by mere inches. Dillingham was not so fortunate, as 7.62mm rounds ripped through his body causing a macabre death dance. A haze of blood filled the air behind him, the back of his head exploding as the last bullet found purchase at the top of his nose. Sarah screamed as the body hit the deck. Metal ripping could be heard coming from the tail of the aircraft as the damaged rotor shredded. Its stability completely compromised, the helicopter began making large lazy circles away from the boat. The orbits began to speed up as it lost altitude, finally smashing into the surface of Tampa Bay. The small explosion was quickly reduced to a burning oil slick as the wreckage sank beneath the waves.

Without a seconds thought, Rob pressed the throttle to full. Sarah was thrown back into the rear seats and Dillingham's body thumped against the bulkhead. The first hint of light was beginning to peek over the eastern horizon. Rob hazarded a glance to the watch on his wrist, which read 5:40. Go baby go, he said to himself nervously steering the boat through the bay.

***

"Alpha-One-Zero-Tango-Zulu-Niner-Bravo-Echo-Echo-Three, Authenticated," the Secretary of Defense replied. Looking at the President, the sandy haired woman asked, "Harold…are you sure about this? I mean, look what you are about to do!" Her pleading eyes began to water as she looked at the President.

"I have no choice!" the President roared. "How the hell do you think I feel? I am condemning three million people to death. THREE MILLION!" He threw the plastic code authenticator onto his desk next to the silver Halliburton case, the black leather pouch having been removed from 'nuclear football'. Bags clung under the Presidents bloodshot eyes as the stress of the last fourteen hours and the responsibility of leadership took their toll. "Admiral," he said to the other man in the room, "as per operation Nero, do not inform the other Joint Chiefs. I order you to carry out operational plan Alpha One per direction of the President of the United States."

"Do not inform the other Joint Chiefs. Carry out operational plan Alpha One per direction of the President of the United States, Aye Sir." the

Admiral responded stiffly and walked out of the command quarters.

"Jennifer," the President said, facing the woman, "I think I want to be alone for this."

A single tear ran down the Secretary of Defense's cheek. "Yes Sir."

The subtle thrumming that was a constant background on the boat seemed to echo in Captain Blake's mind as he reread the Emergency Action Message. Several beads of sweat ran down from his red 'USS Michigan' ball cap. He absently wiped them away with the back of his hand. The CIC seemed stiflingly hot and he repositioned himself under a ventilation duct. Just moments ago, the submarine had received new targeting data for the ballistic missiles, and now this message. He was unaware of any plans to test fire a D5 this patrol, or of any dummy missiles in the load out. In fact, they were en route to do some test firing: torpedoes in AUTEK, not a Trident.

Ordering the Chief of the Boat to call battle stations, Blake took a seat as a flurry of activity erupted around him. The boat exploded to life as all hands took their positions, interrupting everything from training sessions to men trying to get in some rack time before next watch. Several minutes passed while the various stations reported being manned for battle stations.

Blake ordered the boat to launch depth following with the order to hover in preparation for launch. In the Missile Control Center the Weapons Officer ordered missile tube seven open. After further authentication, the launch key safe was opened, extracted, and inserted into the firing panel.

Electricity seemed to fill the air as men sat at their battle stations. Usually, unless personnel were directly involved in the various weapons systems, this was a time to shoot the breeze with their shipmates. The call had come over the 1MC that this was not a drill, and everyone seemed to be filled with a grim determination. Strategic deterrence patrol had just changed to active aggression.

Preparation for launch being complete, the captain waited until the designated time the message had ordered to fire. When the final second ticked by, Blake gave the order to fire. The ship rumbled as the gas generator in number seven-missile tube activated, forcing the missile through the open hatch. Surrounded by a bubble of gas, the missile remained dry until it broke the ocean's surface when the propellant ignited. The internal guidance system took over, directing the missile into a ballistic trajectory toward the target.

***

The events of the evening culminating in the death of one of her superiors in front of her finally overcame Sarah. Rolling to her side, pulling in her legs and wrapping them with her arms, she buried her head and sobbed uncontrollably. The force of her anguish causing her to violently shudder as the boat motored on.

Focusing on their escape, Rob could see the massive Skyway Bridge looming ahead in the growing light. Glancing down, the watch read 5:50. The boat roared between two pylons that marked the end of the channel and headed out toward the open ocean. Minutes later, islands could be seen flanking the channel to the gulf. His watch read 5:58 as he rounded the tip of Ana Maria Island.

At the stroke of six, the boat was traveling the length of the island, when a new sun was born. Where the proud city had once stood was instantly transformed into a wasteland of blackened glass and melted metal. Rob could see his shadow grow as the sunrise came too early. Seconds later, the sound and fury of the blast wave reached the small craft. Sarah screamed in terror as the roar filled the air around them and the boat was tossed about by the pressure wave. The island provided protection from the ferocity of the blast, and Rob said a silent prayer of thanks as he slowed to wrestle the craft back under control. After setting the boat on a course parallel to the shoreline, Rob turned.

An orange and red pillar of fire rose into the sky as its base spread several miles across the landscape. High in the sky, a dark mushroom bloomed in the sky confirming the nuclear destruction. Rob's jaw dropped open involuntarily as he surveyed the storm. "Oh my god" he said quietly in awe of the scene before him. Sarah leaning over the side caught his attention, and he cut the throttle to idle before hurrying to her side. Her body convulsed under the force of her dry heaves. Rob put an arm around her, holding her hair back until she finished and lead her to the front passenger seat. Sitting down, Sarah slumped against the side of the boat as she quietly cried to herself.

"It's going to be alright," Rob said with no conviction.

"Sure," she sniffled. Her face then twisted with anger. "What the hell are we supposed to do now, huh? Where are we going to go? Everybody is dead!" she bellowed. "What is the point?" She then began sobbing again into the seat.

"I don't know." Rob said staring straight ahead. "I guess we just keep going." He pushed the throttle forward fully, racing into their uncertain future.

AKNOWLEDGEMENTS

This book was a long time coming, and it took the assistance of many people to critique and fact check (as much as one can fact check a book about zombies.)

First, I need to thank Donna Bartol and Stephen Ryan for subjecting themselves to the first draft. Their input convinced me that transmission was not a pipe dream and to keep going.

Secondly, I would like to thank SSgt Melissa Scott, TN ANG. Her diligent proofreading helped keep the security forces and Air Force as true as possible.

Next, Dan Civitello, who constantly challenged the stories deus ex machine and keep an eye out for the reader.

Further, thanks go to Cyndi Hill and My wife Misty for the final proofreading. If there are any grammar or punctuation errors, I blame them.

Finally, I need to thank my family for supporting and putting up with me during the arduous writing process.

www.ingramcontent.com/pod-product-compliance
Lightning Source LLC
LaVergne TN
LVHW050618100826
845148LV00011B/1639

* 9 7 8 0 6 1 5 3 5 1 6 5 0 *